BY RICHARD J. LOWE

Box
Repositorium

Shieldmaiden Tales

Fire in the North

Clans of the Silver Hills

Beyond the Sunset Isles

Feybane

RICHARD J. LOWE

Box

Dad
This one's for you

CHAPTER 1

Kevin Maddock made sure the entire work party was in the caged elevator before he closed the gate and slammed his palm on the button that started their descent. The cage rattled and banged its way downwards alongside a large bore water-pipe which ran the length of the main entry shaft. The Mars colony systems were supposed to trap water and recycle it into the treatment plant. However, as the colony grew, the system had become less of a closed loop; wastage, coupled with the increased demand for drinking, washing, and growing vegetables in the agri-domes, kept Kevin and his coworkers in the water mining group very busy.

He turned and looked at his five fellow passengers. He swore when he noticed that number five had some damage on one of its power cables where it connected to the drill servos. Damn it. That was sloppy. He had skipped the systems check on all the autonomous units this morning. That's what you get for saying yes to Dimitri's offer of a quick drink. His friend worked in one of the agri-domes and had access to vegetables that he used to make his infamous homemade rotgut. Christ knows where he had the still hidden. There weren't many places you could get a private moment to yourself, let alone distil ethanol from fermented plants.

The elevator continued to whirr and clunk its way down the shaft. Kevin pushed back the hood of his protective therms as soon as the air warmed enough not to risk frostbite. The surface was too cold to be roaming around in just your coverall; thermal support suits, therms for short, were the martian colonists' answer to their perennial cold weather. At least they didn't have to deal with snow; the martian weather system didn't stretch to that much precipitation yet.

With a none too gentle clattering bump, they came to a halt at the bottom of the access shaft. Kevin opened the cage and stepped out of the elevator.

'All dig-units. Disembark.' A microphone built into his mask picked up his voice and broadcast it from a small speaker.

There was a chorus of bleeps of acknowledgement and the robots' green action LEDs flicked on. Except for number two's. There was a large dent and scuff mark around the housing where the light used to be. They'd run out of replacement bulbs, and it seemed replacement LEDs were a low priority. Since the number of ships making the journey from Earth had dwindled to one every few years, spare parts had been a problem. The colony's fabrication facilities were prioritised to whatever was the flavour of the week for the council. He supposed the water mining operation would shoot to the top of the list if the council members couldn't take a shower.

The last of the robots exited the cage, and he shut the gate with a clang that echoed throughout the underground tunnels.

'All dig-units. Follow me.'

He led his charges down the dimly lit access tunnel. Underground on Mars did not feel as damp as on Earth. Everything was so arid. However, as they proceeded down the tunnel, following the water pipe, he could feel both the temperature and humidity rising until he emerged into the chamber that housed the extraction plant.

Another man, his hood back and therms unzipped at the front looked up from a control panel. 'Hey, Kev.'

'Bannon, how goes it?' Kevin patted the man on the back as he walked past him.

'Been a cave-in in six. One of the digs got a bit bashed up. Laurie's recovering it now.'

'Right.' Kevin took a clipboard from a hook on the wall and checked the work rota. He was down for sector seven today. 'I'd best get started. No rest for the wicked.'

The mine was relatively warm, and the balmy 15 degree centigrade temperature meant Kevin could remove his therms without fear of hypothermia. He still had to wear the mask and the tank-belt around his waist. Pale blue cylinders, the tanks, were fixed to the webbing of the belt and were linked together by short hoses. A longer hose ran from a mixer valve on the belt to his mask and supplied him with air that contained the oxygen he needed. There was an indicator light on the buckle which was currently glowing green indicating the supply was good and reserves were over fifty percent. This would switch to amber when half his tanks were empty and then flash amber when he was down to two. When on the last tank, the light would turn red and an alarm would sound, alerting anyone nearby to his impending suffocation. A constant red light indicated that it was too late, and the tanks had run out of oxygen.

Kevin was supervising his charges from the sector seven control panel. His feet were up on the yellow-painted metal of the panel housing, and he was watching the screens as he occasionally lifted his mask to take a bite out of an oat bar. One flat panel screen was displaying the camera feed from number five. A microphone pickup provided the means for him to issue orders to the dig-units rudimentary AIs. There was also a screen that was displaying status indicators for all the units: tunnel temperatures, a seismograph and other bits of data the engineers who built it thought would be useful. These readouts were showing no problems, and the damaged power cable did not seem to be causing number five any trouble. The drill was boring its way into the rock face, throwing up a haze of dust which made the camera feed a bit pointless.

Kevin had just finished eating his oat bar when several warning indicators for number five all came on at once, and the panel's warning buzzer started to sound.

Kevin swung his feet down, and leaned forward, peering at the display and frowning. He pushed the button which stopped the audible alarm. The indicators were still flashing various shades of red, orange and yellow. Turning his attention to the live camera feed, he saw that the drill had stopped. So much for the power cable lasting until the end of the shift. He confirmed that the other units were all still operational and then gave the order to shut them down.

'All dig-units. Cease operation.'

Then, continuing to follow the stipulated safety procedure for work face access by an operator, he pressed the button which switched off the bucket conveyor that was carrying the water-bearing rock to the extractor.

Once the conveyor had shuddered to a halt, he spent a moment enjoying the silence, then sighed, picked up his toolbox, and headed towards the access tunnel that led to the work face.

By the time he reached dig-unit five, the dust from drilling had settled out of the air, forming a gritty film over the unit.

'Dig-unit five. Isolate drill unit power.'

There was a beep, followed by the click of relays as the unit complied.

'Now, let's have a look—'

Kevin stopped. His eyes were drawn to the rock face and something that shouldn't be there. It was a smooth, gunmetal grey surface. What was left of number five's drill was resting on it, twisted and broken. Kevin hesitated then touched his fingertips to the grey surface. It felt impossibly smooth. None of the grit from drilling had stuck to it at all.

'What the hell?'

He rapped the surface with his knuckles. A dull thunk. Whatever it was, it was solid. Kevin considered bringing another dig-unit over to clear more of the rock, then discarded the notion as another broken drill would be a disaster. He went to his toolbox and fished out a small pick he used for taking rock samples. He looked at it a moment and then considered the rock face. He'd need something bigger and some help.

CHAPTER 2

The sun hung in the sky, casting a wan light over the ruddy landscape. His brush daubed the canvas with swathes of red as he painted the rocky terrain he could see in front of him. Next, he would fill in the pale blue sky. This would take a little longer than it used to; these days there were almost always wispy clouds breaking up the thin blue of the sky. He glanced at his palette. There was even a selection of greens, the most recent addition to the colours required for landscape painting on Mars.

Daniel Maddock had been chronicling the terraforming activity on Mars, via the medium of watercolour landscapes, for over thirty years now. Born and raised on Mars, he was a third generation Martian. In his lifetime, temperature, atmospheric pressure and oxygen levels in these low-lying areas had reached a point where more than just lichen could grow. Now, as well as the yellows and greys of lichen covering the martian rocks, there was a green carpet of bio-engineered moss spreading across parts of the landscape. You still needed a mask outside though. It would be his generation's great-great-grandchildren who would be the first to breathe Martian air directly. That is, unless the work of his daughter and her colleagues came to fruition.

There was a light bonging noise followed by a calm female voice. 'Simone will be arriving within five minutes.'

They still used terrestrial time units on Mars, although a Martian day lasted 24 hours, 37 minutes, and 22 seconds, give or take a microsecond. As Daniel understood it, to prevent massive confusion over what time of day lunch was, standard colony time (SCT) had a twenty-fifth 'hour' which only lasted 37 minutes and 22 seconds.

His daughter, Simone, was part of a team whose goal was to make it possible to play a round of golf on the surface of Mars without needing a mask. 'The Program', as they called it, was concerned with human gene editing to modify the genome of newborn colonists. The idea was for the next generation to have increased lung gas-exchange and their haemoglobin to have an improved delivery capability. The scientists had engineered a mouse that could scurry about on the surface without suffocating; Daniel didn't think it could play golf. Human trials had not yet been given the go-ahead by the colonial council, and he was sure he'd hear all about how short-sighted the council were when his daughter arrived.

'Doris. Coffee please.'

He didn't have to be polite to the hab-AI, but he spent so much time with her, he didn't like to be rude.

'Making coffee,' said the ever calm female voice.

He heard the click of the coffee machine switching on and waited in anticipation for the smell of brewing coffee to fill the habitat. Thank God they had managed to transport viable coffee plant seeds from Earth. In his opinion, of all the crops grown in the agri-domes, coffee was the true success story of Martian agriculture.

The three chimes notifying Daniel someone was at the airlock snapped him out of his reverie.

The hab-AI started to inform him of the obvious. 'Simone is—'

'Yes, yes, I know. You only just told me she was on her way.'

'—at the door.'

'Doris, just let her in.'

There was a buzz followed by a loud clunk as the airlock cycled open. He sipped his coffee, looked out of the window and listened to the sound of the outer door closing followed by a hiss as the pressure was matched with the inside. The final chunky metallic noise of the internal door opening was quickly followed by, 'Hi, dad.'

He swivelled around in his chair and smiled at his oldest child. She was dressed in the ubiquitous grey coverall of the martian colonist, and wore her chestnut brown hair, the same colour as his used to be, tied back in a ponytail. She had hung her therms on one of the pegs in the airlock.

'Simone, come and give your father a hug,' he said, rising to his feet, arms wide and welcoming.

Simone crossed the room, and he folded her into a bear hug. 'You don't come down and see me much these days,' he said, resting his chin on the top of her head.

'I've been busy dad,' said Simone. 'The gene editing project keeps me and Jacob busy, you know that.'

'How is that husband of yours?'

'Oh, he's fine.' Simone pulled back and helped herself to a seat on the battered grey sofa.

'And—'

'And, no, I'm not pregnant yet.'

Was he that predictable? 'Right, yes. Good. I mean, I'm sorry to hear that.'

Simone fiddled with an ancient solitaire set on the table by the sofa, moving the milky marbles from one semi-spherical hollow to another. 'I'm not going to be until the program is ready. The council are stalling. Again.'

'Can't you just have one the old-fashioned way? What's wrong with that?' asked Daniel.

Simone stopped her random marble movement and looked up at him. 'We want our child to breathe the air outside without a mask.'

'Yes, I know. It's kind of hard for me to believe that's going to be possible so soon.'

Simone nodded. 'I know. We've made amazing progress over the last ten years. We're so close, which makes the council's refusal to let us run our trials very frustrating.'

'I'm sure they'll come round. Coffee?'

'Please.'

Daniel poured two coffees and returned to sit in his favourite armchair. It was even more worn than the sofa. It had come with them when they had moved out of the communal hab into one of the private habs. A private hab was one of the advantages of being a council member's family. Simone had offered to replace the chair, but he had gently turned her down. It had been with him since he and Doris had married and reminded him of the happy times they had spent together after Simone had been born and they were allocated a family room. The new hab, he still thought of it as new even though he had been here for over a decade, was larger and, since the accident, lonelier. He'd changed the name of the hab's AI to his wife's name during one drunken evening of lonely misty-eyed reminiscing. He still couldn't bring himself to change it back to the descriptive, but soulless, default 'Habitat-AI'.

'Dad, are you alright?'

'Mmm? Yes, sorry.'

'You spaced out on me for a moment there.'

'Just thinking about your mother, dear.'

'Oh, dad.' Simone came over and sat on the arm of his chair and put her arm around his shoulders. 'I miss her too.'

'What is it they say? She's in a better place now.'

Simone said nothing and just hugged him a little harder. She then stood up and brushed the wrinkles out of her clothes.

Daniel noticed his daughter's eyes were damp. 'Now look what I've done. I've upset you.'

'Don't be silly, dad. I'm just remembering mum too.'

'She'd be proud of you, you know. She really believed in your work.'

'The Program wouldn't have got off the ground without her support on the council.' Simone picked up her coffee and took a sip. 'I do know one thing.'

'What's that?'

'She'd have something colourful to say to the rest of the council.'

'She would, wouldn't she?' Daniel chuckled.

Simone smiled. 'That's better. Less of the frowny face.' She went back to looking slightly concerned. 'I'm sorry. I've not seen much of you lately.'

'Oh, don't worry about me,' said Daniel. 'You two are

busy, I understand that. There'll be plenty of family time when you give me that grandson I've been after.'

Simone laughed. 'You don't give up, do you? Why don't you go hassle Kevin for some grandchildren?'

'Your brother? He's even less likely to have kids.'

'Point taken,' said Simone. 'Maybe one day, he'll look up from the rock face and realise there's more to life than the water mines.'

Daniel raised his eyebrows at this. 'Glasshouses, stones, pots and kettles.'

Simone threw a cushion at him, which seemed to bring the well-worn conversation about grandchildren to a close.

CHAPTER 3

It was two weeks after the council had once again turned down the application for human trials that Simone visited her brother on site. Kevin had found the article describing the decision buried in the depths of the colony news feed. The reporter had spun the story in the council's favour, painting them as protectors of the purity of humanity. He wondered how long it would be before the program was shut down for good. The mining operation in sector seven had been shut down, but this was in the name of science. It seemed that the council had no problems with the study of alien artefacts. Kevin had been assigned to assist the scientists as required, which had mostly involved enlarging the excavation to accommodate the equipment and personnel involved with examining the object.

Kevin and Simone were standing in the area that had been designated the visitor viewing gallery. It was some distance from the object, and a metal handrail had been fitted to denote the start of the restricted area. She had come down after the last work period of the day, so nobody else was around.

'Is it always this warm down here?' asked Simone.

She was looking at her wrist and the temperature reading

on her cuff. These were worn by all colonists, resembled a wristwatch, and, as well as telling the time and the temperature, functioned as a communicator when connected to the colony network.

'Yes. Double-digit Celsius all day long. The rock's a good insulator, so heat generated by our operations here doesn't go anywhere fast.'

'Huh. I never knew.'

Kevin shrugged. 'Why would you?' She had never visited him at work before and probably never would have if it weren't for his discovery.

The object looked like the bottom corner of a giant grey cube, buried in the rock. It was smooth and featureless, and a good five metres of height and width had been exposed. However, it was still partially buried, so they did not know exactly how big it was. They had been going slowly with digging it out, like archaeologists on Earth excavating ancient remains. Actually, Kevin thought, that was exactly what they were doing. They didn't know how old it was or what it was made of as the object had so far resisted all attempts to obtain a sample.

'Can I go down there?' asked Simone.

'You are a scientist. So I guess it's alright,' said Kevin.

He followed Simone down a freshly cut set of stone steps. Kevin admired the clean, precise surfaces. A nice job even if he did say so himself.

'It's amazing.' Simone reached out with her hand as if to touch the object. 'Can I?'

'I don't think anyone will mind,' said Kevin.

Simone touched the flat, grey surface gingerly as if afraid it might be hot. Then, more confidently, she ran her finger down the face of the cube. 'It's so smooth.'

'Weird isn't it?'

'And they don't know how old it is?' asked Simone.

'Nope.' Kevin had to admit, he was enjoying himself. Even though he had no idea what the object was, he liked knowing more about it than Simone.

'Fascinating.' Simone was now pacing around the corner to the side most recently exposed.

'They've not been able to see inside yet. According to their x-ray machines the universe just stops at the outside.'

'Uh, Kev.'

'Yes?'

'What's this?'

Kevin went to join his sister and see what she was talking about. She was pointing at the side of the object which had previously been perfectly smooth. Now there was what looked like a large circle of slightly darker material. It was as tall as Simone and directly in front of her.

'What the hell?' That had definitely not been there earlier when he had helped clear the rock away.

Simone placed her fingers onto the outside of the circular area and started to run them around the edge.

'Careful,' said Kevin.

'It's still smooth. Just a slightly different colour.'

Before Kevin could say anything else, there was a high pitched 'ting', and Simone pulled her hand back sharply. They both took a step back as a black spot appeared in the centre of the dark grey circle. Almost instantly the spot had enlarged until the circle had vanished to be replaced by a hole leading into the inky blackness of the object's interior.

'I don't know about you, but I'm going to need a change of underwear,' said Kevin.

Simone didn't answer. She had taken a step back and was trying to see inside the object without getting too close.

'We should call the team,' said Kevin. He lifted his cuff to make the call.

Simone grabbed his wrist putting her hand over his cuff. 'And miss out on being the first to see inside?'

'So what? What's so great about being first?'

'And that's why you dig holes for a living,' said Simone.

'Dig holes?' Kevin felt slighted by the two-word description of his mining career.

He grabbed his sister's arm as she moved towards the hole. 'What do you think you're doing?'

'Finding out what's inside. You got some light?'

Of course, he did. A flashlight was standard issue down here. He retrieved it from his pocket and twisted the end, sending a beam of light into the hole.

'Can't make out much. Let's get a closer look,' said Simone. She held out her hand expectantly.

'What?' asked Kevin.

'Give me the flashlight. Unless you want to go first?'

Kevin hesitated, then answered her by stepping into the object. He played the light around the interior, picking up several smooth grey surfaces, much like the outside. He felt Simone clutch his arm, she had followed him in.

'This is amazing. What do you think it is?' asked Simone.

'No idea,' said Kevin.

'And why did it open for us?'

'Still no idea.'

There was a light ting – the same noise they had heard

earlier. Kevin spun around, filled with a sudden sense of dread. The hole was gone. Behind them was a solid, featureless grey wall. Then, there was an intense blaze of light, and he had to raise his arm to protect his eyes.

'Kev, what's happening?' asked Simone.

The light dimmed a little, settling at a bearable level. Kevin dropped his eyes and saw Simone blinking as she took in their surroundings: a barren ten-metre square room with walls, floor and ceiling all the same featureless grey as the exterior. They appeared to be prisoners.

'This is bad,' he said.

'Kevin, you have a remarkable skill for stating the obvious.'

Some time passed. Their cuffs had lost connection with the colony network. Kevin had supervised the hardwired connection to an access point in the lab yesterday, but so far the icon indicating that there was no connection stayed obstinately on. Apart from that, the cuffs were working normally; without them, it would have been hard to judge how much time had passed. After four hours, Simone's tank indicator was a constant amber, showing she was below half her supply. Kevin's was also amber but had started blinking. He was on his penultimate tank of oxygen. This was not helping him relax. He was, for the umpteenth time, hammering on the area of the wall they had entered and shouting for help.

'Even if there was anyone there to hear you, and they heard you, how will they get us out?' asked Simone.

'We're going to die in here, Sim. We're going to run out of oxygen and die.'

He gave the wall another smack with the flat of his hand.

'You're just using your air faster,' said Simone.

'What do you suggest? Sit around and wait?'

'Yes. At least until someone who might be able to help is outside. At the moment it's just a couple of your dig-units.'

Kevin sighed and slumped to the ground next to his sister. 'You're right.'

'Of course I am. We have enough air to last if we both share and, this is important, we don't exert ourselves physically.'

'Right.'

'In fact, it would help if we went to sleep.'

'Are you joking? We might never wake up!'

Simone rapped her knuckles on his head. 'Dumbo, set your cuff alarm.'

'Hey, cut that out. I'm feeling a little stressed, okay?'

'Sorry. Besides, your low oxygen alarm will wake you up before it's too late.'

Kevin tried to load his reply to that with as much sarcasm as he could. 'That makes me feel much better.'

'Come on. Let's swap some of your empties for my full tanks.'

Simone started to unclip one of the full tanks from her tank-belt.

'You don't have to do that yet,' protested Kevin.

'Tough. I'm doing it now.'

Simone pushed the oval tank towards him. Reluctantly, he took it and swapped out one of his tanks. They repeated the exercise a couple of times until they both had the same number of full tanks and a steady amber indicator light.

'Now. Sleep,' instructed Simone as she set the alarm on her cuff.

Kevin followed suit, setting the alarm for 07:00 SCT, which was when the scientists would start arriving to continue their observation of the object. He removed his tank-belt and carefully placed it to one side, making sure the tube to his mask was not kinked. Then, he lay down on the hard grey floor and shut his eyes. The tension of their current predicament kept sleep at bay for a while. He lay there listening to Simone's breathing become slow and steady, with the occasional snort of a half snore thrown in for a bit of variety. He couldn't understand how she could get to sleep so quickly. His brain was alive with all possible outcomes in the morning; not many of them were happy endings. Eventually, however, the comforting sound of his sister sleeping soothed him. It reminded him of when they shared the family room back in the communal habitat all those years ago. Slowly he slipped towards sleep.

CHAPTER 4

'Daniel, you have a call from Jacob.'

Daniel didn't look up and continued stippling a light green onto the lower left corner of his canvas.

A few seconds passed before Doris spoke again. 'Daniel, he is quite insistent that he speaks to you.'

Daniel sighed and put down his brush. 'Very well. Doris, put him on speaker.'

'Call from Jacob Aarons,' the AI announced.

Daniel resisted the urge to comment on Doris stating the obvious as Jacob would now be able to hear him.

The disembodied voice of Jacob filled the habitat. 'Hello, Daniel.'

'Hello, Jacob. What is it?'

'Is Simone there?' Jacob's tone had a tinge of desperation to it.

'No, why?'

There was a pause. 'She's missing.'

'Missing?' Daniel sat bolt upright. Nobody just went missing on Mars.

'She didn't make it back to the hab after work yesterday,' said Jacob.

'I'm sure Simone is just visiting friends.'

'She didn't call. And I've checked with everyone I could think of.'

Daniel decided not to comment on the fact that he was the last person Jacob had checked with. 'What about her cuff?'

'The hab-AI doesn't know where she is. Her cuff isn't responding to any pings.'

'You need to call ColPol,' said Daniel. The Colony Police force, ColPol for short, had the security overrides required to perform a comprehensive AI search.

'Yes. Right. I'd better do that now.'

'Call ended,' said Doris.

Daniel didn't pick up his paintbrush. He was worried. The last person to disappear off-net had been murdered by one of his co-workers in an agri-dome, dismembered and then recycled into fertiliser. He shook his head in an effort to rid himself of all the worst-case scenarios vying for his attention.

'Doris, please give me the news feed on screen.'

A large screen mounted on one wall flicked into life. It showed the colony news channel. The news was being read by an AI presenter whose features had been modelled with psychological markers that people instinctively found trustworthy. The current piece was about the artefact that his son had discovered last week. It seemed like the entire colony had been talking about nothing else.

'Doris, switch the screen off but notify me if there is any mention of Simone.'

'Yes, Daniel,' said Doris, and the screen switched off.

Daniel stared at his reflection in the glassy black mirror, his thoughts as dark as the screen.

CHAPTER 5

Kevin was woken by the beeping of his cuff alarm. His back ached, and his bed felt strangely uncomfortable. There was also something on his face. He pawed at his mouth and found that, for some reason, he had gone to sleep with his mask on. Confused, he opened his eyes and then realised where he was.

'Shit.' He stood up and looked down at his sister.

He saw Simone's eyes flutter open. 'Mmm?'

Kevin looked down at his tank indicator as it flicked from a flashing amber light to flashing red, and a strident alarm started to sound. 'Perfect.' He flicked the toggle switch which muted the alarm, then put the tank-belt back on.

Simone sat up and stretched. 'That has to be the worst night's sleep I've ever had. I hate sleeping with this on.' She tapped her mask.

'Well, that's the least of our worries right now.' Kevin gestured at the flashing red light on his belt.

Simone picked up her tank-belt and looked at the indicator. It was flashing amber. She was on her penultimate tank. 'Right.' She put the belt on and stood up. 'We need to let them know we're in here.'

'Any ideas?' asked Kevin.

'Yes.' Simone took out her flashlight and started tapping it on the exterior wall.

'Uh, I tried hitting it last night.'

'You don't know what this is?' asked Simone as she continued hitting the wall with the flashlight.

Kevin listened for a moment, then said, 'Oh! Morse code.'

'If they hear this, they'll know there're people inside.'

'And then what?' asked Kevin.

Simone looked at him questioningly. 'What do you mean?'

'I mean, this thing has resisted all attempts to shave off even a tiny sample. How are they going to get us out?'

Simone shrugged. 'Maybe one of them will touch it and the circle will appear.'

'You know the worst thing about hoping for that?'

'Go on,' said Simone.

'It's the only hope we have.' Kevin leant against the wall next to Simone and slid down until he was in a squatting position. 'So that's it then?'

Simone just carried on tapping out the morse code for 'S.O.S' and looked at him.

'My last moments will be spent listening to you tapping on a wall.'

'Be quiet, little brother,' said Simone. 'You're wasting oxygen.'

Kevin obediently shut up, taking a glance at his oxygen gauge.

The seconds ticked away.

Tap-tap-tap. Tap. Tap. Tap. Tap-tap-tap.

The seconds turned into minutes.

Tap-tap-tap. Tap. Tap. Tap. Tap-tap-tap.

Then, the harsh sound of a tank-belt alarm.

'Shit,' said Simone.

'Hey, that's what I said,' said Kevin, breaking his silence.

Simone toggled the alarm off, stopped tapping the wall and sat down next to Kevin. 'They can't help us, can they?'

'No,' said Kevin.

They sat in silence for a couple of minutes, their belt indicators blinking a baleful red. Kevin used the time to think about all the things he wished he both had and hadn't done with his life. He started with stuff from his childhood, which was quite quick and mostly to do with wishing he'd been nicer to his parents and sister. His adolescence took longer. 'Misspent youth' was a phrase that could be applied to most of it.

'Kev,' said Simone, interrupting his mental bookkeeping of his bad life choices and general lack of achievement.

Kevin turned to look at his sister. She was looking at his tank-belt. He followed her gaze. The belt indicator light was a solid red.

'Apparently, you should've suffocated by now,' said Simone.

'It must be broken.'

'I don't think so.' Simone reached over and lifted his mask off.

'Hey!' Kevin panicked. He grabbed the mask from her hands and rammed it back over his mouth. He struggled for a moment trying to reseat the mask correctly, so it made a seal. Then stopped, confused. He was breathing normally. He dropped the mask.

'Bloody hell,' he observed.

Simone started laughing. It was with a slight touch of hysteria.

'Bloody hell,' repeated Kevin.

Simone ripped off her mask, and giddily announced, between laughs, 'We're not going to die!'

'Of asphyxiation,' said Kevin.

Simone stopped laughing, and her face fell. 'Oh.'

Kevin threw his mask against the far wall where it fell to the floor with a clatter.

'It's dehydration then,' said Kevin.

Now he thought about it, Kevin realised he was very thirsty. His mouth felt gummed up from the night's sleep; he could use a coffee and perhaps some toast. He was really getting into his breakfast fantasy when he saw a patch of the floor in the middle of the room start to distort and appear to rise upwards. He blinked and rubbed his eyes. This didn't make the apparent hallucination stop.

'Can you see that as well?' asked Simone.

Kevin just nodded.

The phenomenon continued for a couple of seconds, the grey material twisting and reforming, until it finally stopped. It now looked, apart from the colour, exactly like one of the tables found in the communal areas of habs. Complete with two chairs.

Simone got to her feet and hesitantly walked over and pulled one of the chairs out.

'It's a chair, Kev.'

'I can see that.'

There was a quiet swishing noise, and Kevin saw a

panel open in the wall on the far side of the room revealing a small alcove. Moments later, he could detect the smell of fresh coffee and toasted bread.

Simone crossed to the opening, then turned around holding a glass coffee pot and a plate of toast.

'Breakfast?' she asked, a slightly deranged grin on her face.

'I was just thinking about coffee and toast,' said Kevin.

'Me too.' Simone put the pot of coffee and plate on the table and sat down.

Kevin scrambled to his feet and joined his sister. The toast was hot and covered in melting margarine.

'Some jam would have been nice,' said Kevin.

'I prefer mine without,' said Simone.

She picked up a slice of toast and held it in front of her. Turning it about with a look of wonder on her face. 'This doesn't make any sense.'

'Let me try some first, it might not be safe,' said Kevin.

Simone bit into the toast with a mouthwatering crunch.

'Or you can go first if you like.' Kevin picked up another slice, one eye on his sister to see if she looked poisoned at all. When he saw she was chewing with obvious relish, he went ahead and bit into his slice. It tasted like it looked. Toasted bread covered in margarine. Now he needed some coffee to wash it down.

'No cups,' said Kevin. He picked up the coffee pot.

'Oh, you're right,' said Simone.

There was another swishing noise from the alcove. They both turned to look and saw two mugs. They were white, one had 'his' written on it and the other 'hers', in blue and pink writing respectively.

Simone dropped her toast. 'What? Those are our cups from home!'

'Really?' asked Kevin. 'A bit twee aren't they?'

'What are my cups doing here?'

'Having my coffee put in them.' Kevin retrieved a cup, the one labelled 'his' of course, and filled it with coffee.

'Seriously. That's Jacob's,' said Simone, pointing at the mug in Kevin's hand accusingly.

'I don't see him about to claim it, so now it's mine. God, this coffee's good.'

Simone stood up and started pacing up and down while she talked. 'Think about this logically.'

Kevin took a noisy slurp from his coffee cup.

Simone continued, apparently interpreting his noisy drinking as agreement. 'This is an alien artefact. Correct?'

'Yup.'

'The air inside is breathable by humans and doesn't appear to have any harmful effects.' She demonstrated by inhaling deeply.

'Agreed.' Kevin wondered where Simone was going with this. Knowing his sister, it was best to not interrupt and only make general noises of agreement.

'When we were hungry and wanting some breakfast, the artefact provided it.'

'And very nice it was too,' said Kevin.

'But not just any breakfast,' said Simone.

'What do you mean?'

'Look. If this artefact is an alien machine, I can get how it might be able to analyse our bodies somehow and determine our requirements. A sufficiently advanced technology could theoretically produce food from its constituent molecules.'

'Like a replicator in that ancient show Dad made us watch.'

Simone nodded distractedly. 'It can provide air in the mix we need to breathe. Food containing nutrients we require. But coffee? And toast, just the way we like it?'

'Hey, speak for yourself. I like jam on mine.'

Simone waved away his objection. 'And these mugs.' She picked one up from the table. 'Not just any mugs, but my mugs. The ones we have in our hab.'

'It is a bit strange, yes.'

'A bit strange? God, Kev. It's like the thing is...' She stopped.

'What is it?' asked Kevin.

Simone continued in a melodramatic whisper, 'Reading our minds.'

Kevin laughed.

'Don't laugh. I'm serious.'

'Sorry, Sim. You're the scientist. Why don't you tell me how real mind reading has turned out to be?'

'Humans reading each other's minds? Complete hokum. Aliens? That's something else,' said Simone.

Kevin had to admit, it would explain the weirdness they had experienced with this morning's breakfast. 'Ok. So it can read our minds and gives us what we think about. I've been thinking about getting out of here on and off since we got trapped and look where it's got me.'

'It obviously wants us in here.'

'Simone, it's a thing. It doesn't want anything.'

'It's probably an AI.'

Kevin snorted. 'AIs don't want anything. They're programmed.'

'Alien,' said Simone.

'Is that how you're going to explain everything?'

'Only the stuff I can't explain,' said Simone.

'Just so I know.'

Simone thought it was reading their minds? Kevin decided to try a little experiment. He closed his eyes and pictured a bottle of Dimitri's rotgut.

'What are you doing?' asked Simone. 'It looks like you're constipated.'

'Thinking about booze. Now, hush, I need to concentrate.'

'Typical.'

Kevin concentrated with all his might for a good ten seconds. He then opened his eyes expectantly. Nothing had appeared.

'Are you done?' asked Simone.

'So much for your theory,' said Kevin.

'Maybe it doesn't work when the substance is harmful.'

'Great. Trapped by an alien member of the temperance movement.'

CHAPTER 6

Daniel lay on his bed, staring at the ceiling. Since talking to Jacob, he had cleaned off the errant paint spatters from near his easel, arranged his brushes by size, and completed a full stock check of his paints. All this had failed to take his mind off the plight of Simone, and he had given up trying to distract himself and decided to just go with lying down and worrying.

The hab AI's voice broke the silence. 'Daniel, there is a story about Simone on the news feed. Do you wish to see it?'

'God, yes.' Daniel instantly got off the bed and moved into the main living area so he could see the screen as it flared into life.

The perfect AI presenter was delivering the news in precise reassuring tones.

'Two people have now been confirmed missing. Brother and sister, Kevin Maddock and Simone Aarons were last seen in the vicinity of the artefact.'

The screen switched to CCTV footage of the pair walking around the half uncovered cube-shaped artefact which Kevin had found. The picture then showed Simone, running her hand in a circle on the surface of the grey, implacable object and a hole suddenly appearing where she had touched it.

As the recording showed the pair gingerly entering the artefact, the AI presenter continued with the report. 'You can clearly see the two entering the object.'

The hole then disappeared as suddenly as it had appeared. Leaving the excavation site empty and lifeless.

'They did not re-emerge and have not been seen since.'

Kevin as well? Daniel felt dizzy; the floor felt as if it was dropping away beneath him. He sat down heavily in his favourite chair; his throat felt choked with emotion, and he had to blink away the tears in his eyes. They were all he had left. This couldn't be happening.

'Scientists have been trying to reopen the object, but have so far failed in this endeavour. We will be running this news item on the hour, and will bring any breaking news as it happens.'

The screen then showed pictures of his children from their colony records. Daniel was numb. It was bad enough Simone being missing. But now Kevin too, and in some alien artefact.

'Doris, I'll be going out for a while. If anyone asks, I'll be at the water mine.'

The hab AI's voice was as even and calm as ever. 'Yes, Daniel.'

Sector seven was crawling with people setting up various pieces of equipment. Daniel assumed it was mostly monitoring equipment, although someone seemed to be setting up some sort of high-powered laser near the artefact which, he had to admit, looked a lot more impressive than it had on the news feed pictures.

Daniel stopped one of the scientists as he was walking past. The man was carrying a clipboard and looked a bit stressed.

'Excuse me, can you tell me who is in charge?' asked Daniel.

'Doctor Webb,' the man said simply. He pointed with his pen towards the machine that was probably a laser. The man fiddling with the machine was familiar to Daniel. He'd seen his picture on the news feed. He was on the council. Simone had mentioned that he was one of those who seemed intent on starving the Program of resources.

Daniel looked from the man and his laser to the massive grey cube half buried in the rock. He supposed they hadn't arranged a replacement for Kevin, who had been in charge of removing the rock from around the site. Hoping that Doctor Webb could give him good news about his two children, Daniel descended the stone steps leading down to the ominous object.

'Doctor Webb?'

The man looked up, pushing a pair of glasses up his nose.

'Yes?'

'I'm Daniel Maddock.'

Webb gave a start of recognition. His surname Daniel supposed. Webb would certainly have known Doris.

'I'm the father of Simone and Kevin.'

Webb frowned. 'And that should mean something to me why?'

'The two people inside that.' He gestured towards the smooth grey surface beside them.

'Oh. I'm sorry.'

'Most people I meet are.' Daniel did not think Webb

sounded that sorry. 'I'm hoping you'll be able to tell me what the hell is going on.'

'If you've seen the news feed, then you know almost as much as us.'

'Are they really inside?' Daniel examined the sheer surface of the object. 'Where does it open?'

'Both good questions,' said Webb. 'The answers are "we think so" and "apparently here".' As he gave the second answer, Webb pointed at a bit of the surface that looked identical to the rest of it. 'If you're about to ask "how does it open?" the answer is we don't know.'

Daniel had been just about to ask that exact question. Instead, he decided to ask about the machine that Webb had been fiddling with. 'Is that a laser?'

'No. It's a quantum projection device. It operates at a subatomic level.'

Daniel was starting to feel the way he did when Simone started to explain her work to her dear old dad.

Webb, apparently detecting the lack of comprehension on Daniel's face, stopped his explanation. 'Yes, it's sort of like a laser.'

'And you're going to use it on that.' Daniel nodded towards the object.

'Yes.' Webb pushed a button on the thing that was sort of like a laser and adjusted a dial. 'And now we should move to a safe distance.'

Daniel hurried to comply, retreating back to the observation area where he was handed a pair of goggles. A warning klaxon then sounded three short blasts, which prompted everyone else to back away from the object and don their own goggles. Webb was holding a small black box with a single switch on it.

'Stand by,' said Webb.

Daniel stood by. He wasn't entirely sure what he was standing by for, but thought he should probably listen to the man with a remote control for something that was sort of like a laser.

Webb flipped the switch.

As far as Daniel could tell, apart from a faint hum from the machine, nothing happened. He looked around. Everyone seemed to be watching the machine and the object expectantly. He shrugged and returned his attention to the scene that was unfolding in front of him. He blinked a couple of times, trying to clear whatever was making his vision blurry, then stopped when he realised that it was only the edges of the artefact which were smearing across his vision.

'Something's happening!' exclaimed one of the observers.

Was it working? Would Simone and Kevin be returned safe and sound? Daniel leaned forward, trying to see what it was that was happening.

The hum from the machine was then matched and drowned out by a deeper pitched humming noise from the object. Then there was a loud, ear-splitting bang, and Daniel's view of proceedings was blocked by a roiling cloud of dust that billowed out across the chamber. He was glad of the filters on his mask as he was engulfed in the powdery rock dust. He wiped his finger across the intake, and it came away caked in dust. He'd need to replace the filters when he got back to the hab.

The dust slowly settled, and what it revealed filled Daniel with a horrible sick feeling in the pit of his stomach. Beyond the machine that was sort of like a laser was a big hole where the object used to be. It, along with Simone and Kevin, had disappeared.

CHAPTER 7

'Did you hear that?'

Kevin looked up at his sister from his makeshift bed on the floor. She was sitting in one of the chairs, her head tilted to one side as if she was listening for something.

'Hear what?' he asked.

'You've spent too much time in the mines, little brother. Your hearing's shot.'

'Can we skip the bit about me ruining my hearing and get to what you heard?'

'It was a popping noise.'

'What, like a balloon?'

'No. Softer, like a soap bubble.' Simone got to her feet and stood very still.

'Now what?'

'Hush. I'm trying to listen.'

Kevin closed his eyes. Simone had given up with her incessant tapping half an hour ago, and he'd been almost enjoying the quiet. He hadn't realised how noisy the environment he lived in was. Obviously, when he was at work, the sound of the dig-units and extraction plant could get pretty loud. When he was back at the communal hab, if there wasn't someone talking then there was the constant background noise of the life support systems: the continual droning of fans moving air around the hab and dripping of water condensers. Even his walks outside were accompanied by the sound of his mask valve feeding him oxygen. This weird grey alien box was refreshingly quiet in comparison.

'Maybe I imagined it,' said Simone.

Kevin opened his eyes and gazed at the grey featureless ceiling. 'It's so drab in here.'

This coaxed a laugh from Simone. 'Drab? Says the man who spends his time staring at rocks all day.'

'You've got to admit that the mine is bright and cheery compared to this.'

Simone looked around at the four bare walls surrounding the solitary table and two chairs. 'I suppose it could use a couple of pictures and maybe a screen.'

As she finished this last sentence, Kevin saw a rectangular section of one of the walls shimmer and then solidify into the distinctive black mirror of an inactive screen.

He sat bolt upright. 'What the hell?'

Simone stood up and stumbled backwards, away from the wall. 'Kev.' She reached for his hand, which Kevin took, gratefully getting as much comfort from his sister as she was from him.

'No way,' said Simone. 'Look at the other wall.' She pointed, her finger trembling.

Kevin tore his eyes away from the screen and looked where she was pointing. There were now two framed pictures hanging on the wall. Not just any pictures. He recognised these as Martian landscapes painted by their father and given as a hab-warming gift to Simone and Jacob when they moved to their married accommodation.

'Let me guess, you were thinking of those paintings,' said Kevin.

Simone just nodded, apparently unable to speak.

'I don't get it,' said Kevin. 'Why does it work for Dad's paintings, but not Dimitri's hooch?'

'Not the best time for joking, Kev.'

'I'm serious. Kind of. It only seems to be you who can bend this crazy grey prison to your will.'

Simone said nothing, her brow furrowed in thought.

'Me? I've been wishing for a pillow for at least half an hour. And booze for longer. Do I get anything? No. Nothing for poor old Kev. But Simone, oh she's special. She's got the power—'

'Kev,' interrupted Simone.

'What?'

'You're babbling.'

'Sorry. It must be the thought of spending the rest of my life in this box getting to me.'

'Don't think like that,' said Simone.

'Why not? It's true isn't it?'

'Think for a moment. Our situation has already improved over the last ten minutes.' She gestured at the screen on the wall.

'What use is a screen? Even if it works, what good will it do us?'

'Why do you think it doesn't work?' asked Simone.

Kevin scrambled to his feet. If Simone was right, and this thing was run by an AI, he'd try talking to it like an AI. 'Box, show the colony news feed.'

Nothing happened.

Simone frowned. 'Let me try something.'

'Be my guest.' Kevin bowed theatrically and extended his arm towards the lifeless screen.

'Box.' Simone stopped. She licked her lips.

Kevin tried not to show his annoyance. 'Go on then, what are you waiting for?'

'Box, show an exterior view.'

The screen flicked into life. It was not, however, showing the chamber outside the box. Instead, the picture was of a row of cubes identical to the one they were in now. These were not buried in rock but were arranged neatly in a gleaming white chamber bigger than any structure on Mars.

'If that's an exterior view, we're not in the water mines,' said Kevin.

Simone looked at him, and he could see fear vying with wonder and curiosity on her face. 'We have to go outside and take a look.'

'How? We're trapped in here, unless you forgot. And even if we did get out, what are we going to breathe?'

'You're right. We mustn't rush into anything.'

Kevin recognised Simone's expression. It was the same one she had worn as a child when determined to get her own way. So, he did what any little brother would do in similar circumstances: he gave in to the inevitable. 'Ok, what do we do then?'

'We start testing my superpowers,' said Simone with a smile.

Kevin laughed. 'Have you thought of a superhero name yet? The amazing box-controlling woman, although accurate, doesn't have much of a ring to it.'

Simone struck a classic superhero pose, hands on her hips and chest puffed out. 'Just call me... Miss Incredible.'

'Alright, Miss Incredible. Work your magic,' said Kevin, still laughing.

'Box, display external atmospheric gas percentages,' said Simone.

The screen flicked to a new display. It was a list of gases and percentages. It was a Nitrogen/Oxygen mix. 17.43% was a lower concentration of oxygen than they were used to but was enough to breathe without a mask.

'How the hell is that even English?' asked Kevin.

Simone had a stupid grin on her face. It was the same grin she used to use when she'd aced a test at school. 'I think I'm getting the hang of this.'

'No shit.'

'We can breathe out there,' said Simone.

'And that helps us how?'

'Box, open a door to the outside.'

A circular hole in one of the walls, identical to the one they had entered yesterday, snapped into existence. Through it, they could see the place that had been pictured on the screen. The row of sombre grey cubes looked more imposing viewed from here.

Simone put her hand on Kevin's shoulder. 'Shall we?'

'What if it closes and we can't get back in?' asked Kevin.

'Ignoring the fact that all we've wanted to do for the past day is get out of here?'

'We weren't considering stepping out into god knows where without any way of getting home.'

Simone nodded. 'Point taken. How about you go out and we see if it closes. I should be able to open it again.'

'Fair enough.' Kevin gingerly stepped through the hole and onto the floor outside. The flooring gave a little as he stepped on it as if it was made from some sort of rubber. Kevin looked back at his sister. 'So far, so good.'

'Yes. Move a bit further away.'

Kevin complied and started to walk towards the row of giant grey cubes in front of him.

'It's still open. I'm coming out too,' called Simone.

Kevin turned and watched his sister step out of the hole. A few metres to her right, a one-metre square section of the cube was covered in a seething, shiny metallic globule. It looked a bit like a giant blob of mercury. A giant blob of mercury that was pulsating and writhing on the surface of the cube. 'What is that?' said Kevin, pointing at the blob.

Simone backed away from the new anomaly and joined Kevin at what he hoped was a safe distance. The metallic blob didn't change its behaviour and simply remained where it was, oozing on the surface of what Kevin had begun to think of as their grey cube.

'Do you think it will go inside?' he asked.

'I'm not sure, but just in case: Box, shut the door.'

The hole closed as quickly as it had appeared.

'I hope you can open it again,' said Kevin.

Simone gave him a sideways glance. She was keeping her attention on the metallic blob. 'Let's find out. Box, open the door.'

The hole reappeared with a light tinging noise.

Kevin let out a sigh of relief. 'Probably best to shut it again.'

Simone nodded and gave the command to shut the door again. As before, the hole closed.

The evenly spaced row of cubes opposite their grey

cube stretched into the distance in both directions. Their box also stood in a row of its own. The two rows stayed perfectly parallel for as far as Kevin could see. It was hard to gauge distance because apart from the cubes, everything was the same, sterile, bright white.

'Where's the light coming from?' asked Simone.

Kevin realised there did not appear to be anything which was a light source in the smooth white of the walls, ceiling and floor. In fact, it was hard to tell where one started and the other began.

'Beats me. Must be because of aliens.' Kevin used Simone's explanation for something that looked like magic.

'Touché,' said Simone.

'Hey, do you think you can open one of the other alien thingies?'

Simone shot her brother a withering look. 'Thingies? Really? Can you please call them cubes or boxes. Actually, I like box, let's go with that.'

'Sorry. Simone, do you think you can open one of the other alien boxes?'

'Better.' Simone strode up to the nearest box. 'Box, open the door.'

Nothing happened.

'Box, open the door,' repeated Simone. This time louder.

Nothing continued to happen.

'That'll be a no, then,' said Kevin.

'If we can't have a look around another box, then we should see what's at the end of the row,' said Simone.

'How will we find our box again? Are you just going to wander up and down the line shouting "open" at them?'

'Good point.' Simone opened the door again and retrieved their tank-belts from inside, dumping them on the floor in front of the box. 'They're empty anyway. May as well use them as a marker.'

Satisfied they'd be able to find their way to this particular box, the pair picked a direction at random and started walking between the rows of implacable grey cubes.

CHAPTER 8

Daniel held his coffee cup, letting it warm his hands. Jacob was sitting on a battered grey sofa nursing his own cup. The two men had found each other at the dig site and, after spending the rest of the day watching impotently as the scientists failed to make the artefact reappear, they had made the trip back to Daniel's hab. Jacob couldn't face going back to the communal hab so when Daniel had offered him the couch for the night, he had readily agreed.

Daniel numbly watched the steam curling out of his cup. They hadn't said a word since getting back, except for Daniel instructing the hab AI to make coffee.

Jacob cleared his throat. Daniel looked up at his son-in-law.

'There's something you should know,' said Jacob.

Daniel remained silent.

'It's just…' Jacob stopped, straightened his shoulders, and started again. 'Simone wanted to be the one to tell you, but—'

'Tell me?' Daniel echoed in incomprehension.

'Tell you, yes. But she can't now, so I have to.'

'Tell me what?'

'We—she's pregnant.'

'Pregnant?'

'Yes. You know the council didn't approve human trials?'

Daniel nodded his acknowledgement.

'Well, we—' Jacob ran his fingers through his hair. 'We couldn't wait any longer, so we edited our son.'

'You edited your son?' Daniel continued echoing what Jacob was saying.

'Increased lung capacity, haemoglobin transfer, a little extra cognitive ability for good measure. The works.'

'Holy shit,' observed Daniel.

'We implanted the embryo a week ago.'

'I'm going to be a grandad,' said Daniel.

Jacob smiled briefly. 'Yes, she knew you'd like that.'

'Oh, God.' The reality of the situation suddenly hit home. His daughter. His beautiful, intelligent, talented daughter was going to give him a grandson. Except that she wasn't. She'd gone. Vanished in an ancient martian artefact to god knows where. And his son, Kevin. All his family, gone. His eyes started to moisten with tears. He felt a thick lump forming in his throat. 'They'll figure out how to get them back, won't they?'

Jacob looked away and said nothing.

* * *

It was the start of their shift. Reims and Conway were divesting themselves of their belts and therms when Reims got the call from the chief. She said they would be right there, sighed, and put her tank-belt back on the rack.

She patted her partner on the shoulder. 'Chief wants to see us, Conway.'

Conway groaned and racked his tank-belt next to hers. 'What about?'

'Something at that dig site.'

'Dig site?'

'Jesus, Conway. Do you live in a goddamn cave?'

'I've been busy,' said Conway.

'They found an alien artefact in the water mines. Now Webb and his mob are crawling all over it doing science shit.'

'Oh.' Conway looked genuinely surprised.

Reims didn't know how he'd done it, but Conway had somehow managed to avoid the news story that had been dominating the colony news feed for the past few days.

'Conway, you are truly one of a kind.'

'Gee, thanks Reims,' said Conway.

Chief Smith was waiting for them in his office. He was the only ColPol officer in the building with a private office. Everyone else was crammed into an open common space to leave more room for interview rooms and overnight holding cells.

Smith tapped the cover of a black folder on the desk in front of him. 'Nice of you two to join me. Sit down.' He indicated the two chairs on the other side of his desk.

Conway sat down and tried to hide his coffee cup.

Reims lifted her cup so Smith could clearly see it. 'We had to stop for essential supplies.'

'I expect you to drop everything when I call.'

Reims sat down and slurped noisily from her cup.

'Sorry sir,' said Conway.

Smith fixed Reims with a glare before continuing. 'I'm

sure you've both heard about the disappearance of the artefact yesterday.'

Reims nodded. Conway looked down at his coffee.

Smith opened the folder and looked at the first page. 'Doctor Webb is convinced that Simone Aarons and Kevin Maddock deliberately absconded with it.'

That didn't seem all that likely to Reims. 'Really?'

'Really. What I need you to do is bring in their family and known associates for questioning.'

Reims nodded slowly. 'Standard shakedown. Got you.'

Smith hadn't finished. 'The good doctor has also reported that Mrs Aarons is also guilty of an unlicensed gene-edited pregnancy.'

'Is that even a crime?' asked Reims.

'It is now.' Smith closed the folder and tossed it over towards Reims and Conway.

Conway grabbed it before Reims had a chance to react. Figured, thought Reims. The guy was born for paperwork.

'We're on it sir,' said Conway.

'Good. This is top priority. As of now those two are the colony's most wanted.'

CHAPTER 9

'That is amazing,' said Simone.

Kevin had to agree. They had walked for fifteen minutes between the rows of boxes before they could see where the multitude of grey cubes came to an end. Another fifteen minutes and they reached an end wall of what they realised was a massive chamber. Fortunately, this wall was not as featureless as the rest of the chamber, and as they approached it, they could see a large semicircular portal blocked by a shimmering blue light. Exactly how large had not been apparent until they got closer and could see it was twice as tall as one of the cubes and, due to its semicircular nature, four times as wide.

'Amazing,' said Kevin. 'How do we get through?'

Simone didn't answer as she paced the length of the curtain of blue light.

'Sim?'

'There's something here,' said Simone. She was at one end of the portal, pointing at something on the wall.

Kevin ambled over to take a look. It was a thirty-centimetre square panel. It was notable in that it was not the same clean uniform white as the rest of the chamber, but was the same grey as the cubes. As he got closer to the light, he could hear a low pitched, almost inaudible, hum.

'What do you think that is?' asked Kevin.

'It's must be to do with opening this.' Simone gestured at the shimmering curtain of blue light.

She slapped her hand palm first onto the panel.

Nothing happened.

'Not just a simple switch, then,' said Simone.

Kevin realised she was talking to herself. He remembered her doing the same thing when figuring out puzzles when they were children. He used to tease her about it but wisely decided not to now.

'I don't suppose you have any tools on you?' asked Simone.

'Just the flashlight, and a panel access tool,' said Kevin. He never went anywhere without the small tool he used to open access panels on the dig-units.

'Door, open,' said Simone.

Nothing happened.

'Looks like your superpowers have failed you,' said Kevin.

'Give me your access tool.' Simone held out her hand.

Kevin fished a small black rod that had a tiny hook on the end out of his pocket and placed it in Simone's outstretched hand. The bespoke tool was only marginally easier to use than a screwdriver but had the added advantage of not damaging the casing on the robot's access panels. He'd had this one since he'd started his job in the water mines. Simone threw it at the barrier.

'Hey!' said Kevin.

The tool hit the shimmering blue light and bounced back, clattering to the floor at Simone's feet.

'That's my bloody access tool,' said Kevin.

She bent down, picked the tool up, and turned it over in her hand, scrutinising it.

'Do I come into your lab and start throwing test tubes about?' grumbled Kevin, not expecting an answer or any contrition from his sister.

He wasn't disappointed. Simone simply tossed the tool back to him. Kevin caught it and inspected it for any damage. 'Lucky for you it's ok.'

'Stop being a baby. I wanted something to test the barrier with that wasn't my hand, and we're not exactly flush with equipment.'

Simone approached the barrier and slowly reached out her hand towards it.

'Wait? What are you doing?' Kevin lunged forward and grabbed his sister by the shoulder, pulling her arm back.

Simone rounded on him. 'Look. I get that you want to protect me, and that is very sweet, little brother. But you saw the tool; it's fine. I'll be fine.' She shrugged his hand off and pushed her hand onto the barrier.

When her hand didn't explode, disintegrate, or catch fire, Kevin relaxed a bit. He was still tense with vague worry in general, but the barrier of blue light did not seem to be dangerous.

'Sorry,' said Kevin. 'It's been a bit of a weird day, and I'm having a little trouble adjusting.'

Simone made her hand into a fist and thumped the barrier a few times. 'I don't think we're getting through that any time soon.' She stood contemplating the barrier for a moment more before turning and marching back the way they had come. 'Come on, let's check out the other direction.'

Kevin, having nothing else to do and nowhere else to be, followed.

Their box hadn't moved. The pair of tank-belts were still in the same untidy pile in front of it, but the metallic blob was gone, leaving the grey box looking identical to its companions. Kevin had noticed that there were a few gaps in the rows of regularly spaced boxes and wondered where the missing boxes were. He also wondered where they were.

'Where do you think we are?'

'You mean celestially, because we sure as hell aren't on Mars,' said Simone.

'What makes you say that?'

'The gravity is wrong. I can feel it, can't you?'

Kevin nodded. She was right. He had been feeling slightly heavier than usual ever since they had stepped outside the box.

'This isn't Mars, and it isn't Phobos or Deimos. This implies a couple of things. First, we are a long way from home. Second, that the box can move faster than the speed of light.'

'Oh,' said Kevin. Simone's reasoning simultaneously filled him with a sense of wonder and terror.

After half an hour of walking, they came across a box that was almost entirely covered in patches of the metallic blob substance that had been on their box. Where they could see the surface of the box, they could see it was blackened and pitted. He wondered what could have damaged the surface like that as it had resisted all attempts to take even a small sample back on Mars.

'Those blobs are probably some sort of automated repair system,' said Simone.

Kevin agreed. It did seem more likely than his initial guess of 'killer space slug'.

They continued walking for another half an hour until they came to another blue barrier at the other end of the chamber. This put the chamber at several kilometres long. It was immense.

After a few minutes of fruitless prodding and poking at the barrier and its attendant control panel, they decided to head back to their box and see if they could still get inside.

As they approached the untidy pile of tank-belts, Kevin's nerves started to jangle with apprehension. This feeling suddenly converted to a wash of relief after Simone's command 'Box, open the door' worked, and the round aperture pinged open allowing them inside.

The table and chairs were still where they'd left them, along with the remains of their breakfast.

'What do we do with that lot?' Kevin gestured at the dirty crockery, inexplicably overcome by the desire to tidy up. 'I don't see a handy dishwasher.'

'No, there isn't,' said Simone. 'But I bet there could be.'

'Right. Superpowers.'

'Box, a dishwasher if you please.' She pointed at the wall.

'You're being polite to it? You get more like Dad every time I see you.'

Simone shot him a look that told him to shut his smart-ass mouth. Kevin was about to elaborate when the section of wall she had pointed to swirled and flowed into what looked remarkably like a dishwasher door. 'I've said it before, but I'll say it again. Bloody hell.'

Simone lifted her index finger to her mouth and blew away some imaginary smoke.

Kevin opened the newly formed door and, sure enough, the inside was unmistakably the internals of a dishwasher. He stared at it a moment, shrugged, put the breakfast things into the rack, then shut the door.

CHAPTER 10

Daniel was roused from sleep by a commotion from the main living area. Groggily, he wondered what Jacob was up to, then he heard unfamiliar voices from next door and snapped awake.

'Doris, who is in the hab?' he asked while he hurriedly pulled on some clothes.

'Current occupants of the hab are Daniel Maddock, Jacob Aarons, Colony Police Officer Lucy Reims, and Colony Police Officer Adrian Conway.'

Daniel's blood ran cold. Thoughts tumbled through his mind: Why were ColPol here? It must be bad news. Please don't let it be bad news.

He zipped up his colonist's coverall and pushed open the door into the main living area of the hab. Jacob was sitting on the sofa. A ColPol officer, wearing the distinctive navy blue coverall of the Colony Police, stood with his arms behind his back. Sitting in Daniel's favourite chair was another member of ColPol. This one had her cap in her hand and was talking earnestly with Jacob.

Daniel imagined the worst. What was actually going on, while not informing the next of kin of Simone's demise, was not good.

'You understand that officer Conway and myself have to take you into custody, Jacob,' said the officer who was sitting down. Daniel surmised that this must be Colony Police Officer Lucy Reims.

Jacob just nodded. He looked shell-shocked.

The door banged shut behind Daniel. Everyone looked his way.

'Ah. Mister Maddock. Do join us, please.' Officer Reims gestured to the sofa.

'You're in my chair,' said Daniel. He wasn't sure why he'd said that.

The ColPol officer's brow furrowed. 'What?'

'You're sitting in my chair.'

She looked down at the chair, then back at Daniel. 'Yes, I am. Now, please take a seat next to your son-in-law. Don't make me ask again.'

Daniel hastily complied. He was still a bit befuddled from being asleep and wasn't really sure what was going on.

'Mister Maddock, I would like to invite you to come with us and help us in our enquiries.'

Daniel looked at the ColPol officer in incomprehension. 'What?'

'Your son and daughter are both wanted in connection with unlawful appropriation of colony property.'

That didn't make Daniel feel any less confused.

'Your daughter is also wanted on a separate charge of unlicensed gene-edited pregnancy.'

Daniel's confusion was replaced by sick dread. 'I don't know—'

'We will find out what you do and don't know back at the police unit, Mister Maddock.'

Officer Reims got to her feet and motioned for Daniel and Jacob to do the same. Daniel stood, suddenly lightheaded. The whole situation was surreal and there seemed to be nothing Daniel could do to avoid being swept along by the tide of events.

He remained in a daze as he donned his therms, left the hab and was shepherded into the back seat of the ColPol rover parked outside. The roads around the Mars colony were made of compacted rock which was perpetually covered in a thin layer of red dust. Attempting to clear the dust was futile as the regular dust storms refreshed this layer almost as soon as it was cleared. The rover threw up a plume of this dust as they drove to their destination.

Daniel was not entirely sure what enquiries he was going to assist with. He understood the charge of unlicensed gene-editing, but he didn't know what he could say that ColPol did not already know or could get from Jacob. As for the other charge: 'unlawful appropriation of colony property', he had no idea what that could be about.

They arrived at the ColPol building after around fifteen minutes of driving. It was squat and made of steel and concrete. Like all older colony buildings, the exterior was pitted and scoured by the power of the storms that had raged across the planet's surface during early terraforming. The storms that now swept across the surface of Mars, although as frequent, no longer had quite the same destructive power. The storm shutters were currently open, but the tinted black windows revealed nothing of the interior.

The airlock was of an older design to the one in Daniel's hab and was much larger, able to accomodate an entire squad of ColPol officers if required. The hiss of gas exchange was loud. It sounded like the valve needed replacing, thought Daniel. Once the green light indicating a breathable atmosphere illuminated, they proceeded into the entry room.

Another officer was sitting behind a desk. He looked up from his screen, watching as they removed their masks, tank-belts and therms. Jacob and Daniel put their thumbprints to a reader to acknowledge transfer of their outdoor equipment before handing them over to the desk officer.

The interview room he was hustled into was small; more of a cupboard than a room, it barely had space for the table and two chairs inside. The furniture was old and dilapidated which matched what he had seen of the ColPol building so far. A beige folder was on the table.

Officer Reims took the chair opposite Daniel. 'Pol-AI, record interview of Daniel Maddock.'

A ceiling speaker tucked into a corner of the room crackled into life. The voice was female and devoid of any emotional inflection. 'Acknowledged, officer Reims. Recording interview of Daniel Maddock. Date and time-stamp applied.'

Officer Reims did not waste any time on pleasantries. 'Did your son tell you he was going to steal the artefact?'

'Steal? What are you talking about?' This was a new slant on events.

She picked up the folder and leafed through the pages. 'Your son is regularly in contact with you. There was a logged call from the Delaney communal hab the day before the theft.'

'How can you call that a theft?'

'Mister Maddock.' Officer Reims put the folder down

58

in front of her. 'We have camera footage clearly showing Kevin Maddock and Simone Aarons taking control of the artefact.'

'Taking control? They didn't come back out!'

She returned to the folder, turning to a page which had a picture of Simone at the top. It had been taken a few years ago, back when she had shorter hair.

'Simone Aarons is also wanted for unlicensed gene-editing, along with her husband and accomplice Jacob Aarons. And he was found at your hab.' Reims leant back in her chair before fixing Daniel with an accusatory gaze. 'Is he the ring-leader?'

'Ring-leader? This is nonsense. Kevin and Simone would never do anything like that.'

'So, Jacob would?'

'No, I didn't say that.'

'The thing is, Mister Maddock, they did abscond with the artefact, and Simone Aarons is carrying an unlicensed gene-edited foetus. You are wasting your time if you are trying to convince me they aren't guilty.'

'The pregnancy. That's real,' admitted Daniel.

'That's better. We're getting somewhere. How long have you known about the unlicensed gene-editing?'

'I only found out yesterday, when Jacob told me.'

'Of course.' Officer Reims pulled out another sheet of paper from the folder and tapped it with her finger thoughtfully. 'When did you find out about the plan to steal the artefact?'

'I don't know anything about any plan,' said Daniel.

'Repeating a lie does not make it so, Mister Maddock.'

'You've got to believe me, there is no plan,' said Daniel.

'There is no plan or you don't know anything about the plan. Which is it Mister Maddock?'

'Neither. Uh. Both.'

'Very well Mister Maddock. Pol-AI, terminate interview.'

The speaker crackled into life with the acknowledgement – 'Interview terminated.'

Officer Reims stood and picked up the folder. 'We will give you some more time to think about it in a detention cell.'

Another blue clad officer entered and escorted Daniel out of the interview room. He was being led to the cells when there was a raised voice from the direction of the main airlock.

'Get your hands off me, I know the way.' The voice was male and aggressive. Daniel thought he recognised it, but wasn't sure until he saw the speaker. It was Dimitri, one of Kevin's friends.

When Dimitri saw Daniel he called over – 'Hey, Danny. What the hell's going on?'

Daniel answered with a shrug as the big man was taken into the interview room.

'Move it, Maddock,' said a ColPol officer, putting a hand on his arm.

'Sorry,' said Daniel.

He allowed himself to be led away to the detention cells. These were small concrete boxes with doors that locked on the outside. His escort presented his cuff to the pad next to one of the cells. This disengaged the lock, allowing the officer to open the cell door and push Daniel inside. There was a solid clicking noise behind him as the lock engaged.

It didn't take long for Daniel to take stock of his new quarters. A hard looking bed and a white plastic toilet were the only furnishings. A solitary light embedded in the ceiling illuminated the cell. He couldn't see a light switch and, although there was a speaker grille above the door, he doubted the AI was listening for his commands; the light was probably on a timer. A single yellow line was painted on the floor bisecting the tiny room. There was no clue to its purpose.

His stomach growled and Daniel remembered that he hadn't had any breakfast. He hadn't even had a cup of coffee. Feeling more than a little sorry for himself, Daniel lay down on the bed and stared at the ceiling. It wasn't long until he started to worry about Kevin and Simone. He was pretty sure that ColPol's theory about a plot to steal the artefact was nonsense, but, in a way, he almost wanted it to be true. The alternative was that they had been abducted by something alien. And that thought gave him no comfort at all.

CHAPTER 11

Kevin and Simone were blissfully unaware of the events unfolding in the Mars colony. They had been experimenting with what the Box could do. The most important thing, as far as Kevin was concerned, was that Simone could ask the Box to follow somebody else's verbal commands. Simone could make things happen by thinking hard enough about them, but it was easier when she vocalised the request as if she was talking to a colony AI. Kevin, although he couldn't just make things happen by wishful thinking, could now use voice commands with the Box. Kevin was currently sitting with his feet up on a battered grey sofa which looked remarkably like the one in their father's hab. Apparently he could only ask for food or drink that Simone had experience of. He had tried for a bottle of Dimitri's hooch, but the bottle that had appeared in what Simone had dubbed the creation compartment (Kevin's suggestion of 'magic cupboard' had been overruled) was wine made from colony-grown grapes. Experimentation had also shown that Simone also needed to hear Kevins request unless it was something he had asked for before. Several bottles of wine on the floor beside the sofa were testament to Kevin's attempts to procure something that wasn't chardonnay.

'You couldn't have tried some hard liquor at least once in your life?' asked Kevin. He took a swig from the bottle of wine that he was holding.

'Some of us have a little bit of concern for our internal organs,' said Simone.

'Bet you're fun at parties.'

Simone made no comment and sipped her water.

'So, we have air, food, drink and a bathroom.' Kevin pointed the wine bottle at a door on the far side of the room. Simone had asked the Box for a bathroom when they had got back from their exploratory walk, the morning's coffee having made its way through their digestive systems. 'Now the only danger is dying from terminal boredom.'

'Perhaps. For the moment, more experiments will keep us busy.'

'More? I thought we were done.' Kevin hoisted his wine bottle towards Simone then took another slug.

'We have a pretty good handle on the fabrication capabilities of the Box. For instance, your request for a rover failed. Probably a size issue.'

'It made the bathroom,' Kevin pointed out.

'Extruded from the fabric of the Box. Not a discrete object. We don't know how much raw material is available for construction.'

Kevin nodded towards the bathroom. 'We don't know where our waste is going either.'

'Probably back into raw materials. This fabrication technology can construct molecules to order, it must have the ability to break them down into constituent elements too.'

'So our food could be made from our waste?' Kevin peered into his wine bottle suspiciously. 'Lovely.'

'Once it's been broken down, it ceases being, uh, waste,' said Simone.

Kevin swung his legs down from the sofa and leaned back, stretching his arms out across the back of the sofa. 'Fascinating. You're not planning experiments with our poo are you?'

'No. We need to see if we can get the Box to travel.'

'Travel? You mean go home?' Kevin hadn't thought of that.

'Yes. The trick will be working out what to visualise.'

'Just think of home, surely.'

Simone gave him a condescending look. 'First thing I tried. Nothing.'

'Oh.' Kevin's excitement faded. 'Maybe it's not possible.'

'Maybe. But it's not like I've got anything else to do is it?'

'What do I do?'

'I don't know, catch up on your reading?'

'Not a bad idea. Box, make me an e-reader.'

The door of the creation compartment slid open to reveal what looked like a standard issue colony e-reader. Kevin walked over, picked it up and depressed the on switch. The display came to life.

'Oh,' said Kevin.

'What is it?' asked Simone.

'There's no books on here.' The e-reader's inventory was empty.

Simone laughed. 'I suppose there couldn't be.'

'You're telling me that the Box can make a working e-reader, but can't rustle up something to read?'

'Technology obeys the universal laws of physics. Stories on the other hand' – Simone tapped her temple with a forefinger – 'they're the domain of the imagination.'

'Bugger,' said Kevin. He threw the useless e-reader on to the sofa and sat down heavily next to it. 'I'm guessing an entertainment unit would have no movies or games on it?'

'Go ahead and try,' said Simone.

Kevin spent the next ten minutes growing a pile of functional but content devoid electronic entertainment devices.

'Have you quite finished?' asked Simone as she watched Kevin throw a gamepad at the wall in frustration.

'Yeah. Looks like the only entertainment around here is drinking and creating a pile of useless electronic crap.' He kicked said pile of useless electronic crap, causing a minor avalanche of games consoles that spilled across the floor.

'I hope you're going to tidy that lot up,' said Simone.

'Where to?' asked Kevin.

'Box, give us waste disposal,' said Simone.

A new door flowed into being next to the creation compartment. This one was labelled 'Waste Disposal'. Kevin noticed the original compartment was now labelled with the name Simone had chosen for it.

'Cute,' said Kevin.

Opening the door revealed an empty grey compartment identical in appearance to its neighbour. He then proceeded to fill it with his pile of useless electronics. Once he had finished, he slid the door shut and there was a whooshing noise. Re-opening the door revealed the compartment was now empty with no evidence of anything ever being inside.

'They'd kill for this recycling tech back home,' said Kevin.

'About that,' said Simone.

Kevin raised an eyebrow and looked at his sister quizzically. 'Recycling?'

'Home.'

'What about it?'

'We should see if we can make the Box go places. Home for instance.'

'We don't know where we are,' said Kevin.

'I don't think I need to.'

'Right. Mind reading alien box.'

'Box, travel home,' ordered Simone.

As far as Kevin could tell, nothing happened.

'Let's see if that worked,' said Simone. 'Box, show an outside view.'

The screen flicked into life, showing the now familiar sight of a row of other alien cubes.

'Bugger,' said Kevin, with feeling.

Simone was quiet for a moment. Kevin could tell she was thinking by the faint frown wrinkling her forehead. 'I was thinking of the concept of home. What if this is the Box's home?'

'Oh. I see. Maybe you need to be a bit more specific?'

'Right. Box, travel to our home.'

The screen went momentarily dark, then a new picture was displayed. The sun must be behind them as a large square shadow was being thrown against a rocky cliff face.

'Looks like it worked,' said Kevin.

'Wonder where we are?'

'One way to find out,' said Kevin. 'Box, open the—'

'Wait.' Simone interrupted him.

'What?'

'We need our masks,' said Simone.

Kevin gestured at the tank-belts which were lying by the sofa. 'They're empty, remember.'

'No problem. Magic alien box, remember?'

Simone quickly ordered up a refill point next to the dishwasher and they spent a few minutes re-gassing their tanks. Once they were full, they donned their therms and masks and got ready to leave.

'Box, open the door,' said Kevin. This time Simone did not interrupt him and the round egress point opened in front of them.

They stepped out into sweltering heat. Kevin's limbs felt leaden. He felt like he was walking through treacle, and could already feel sweat starting to prickle his skin in the heat.

'Bloody hell,' said Kevin as he quickly undid the front of his therms.

'What?' Simone looked as confused as he was.

He could see her shoulders visibly drooping. Simone was obviously feeling the same pull downwards that he was.

'This is not Mars,' said Kevin, stating the obvious. If they had been on Mars in the shade, they would have felt the chill through their therms. This temperature was ridiculous, it must be at least 25 degrees centigrade.

'Back inside,' said Simone.

Kevin nodded his assent, and they retreated back inside

the Box, escaping the heat and the weird pull downwards. While Kevin stripped off his therms, Simone called up a display of the atmospheric gas percentages outside the Box.

'Kevin.' Her voice was trembling.

'What?' He looked at the screen.

'This is an Earth normal atmosphere. Look, 20.946% oxygen. That's a match to three decimal places. So is the nitrogen. Even the noble gases.'

'How do you remember that stuff?' said Kevin.

Simone ignored the question, instead sharing her conclusion with him. 'It's Earth Kev. The Box has taken us to Earth.'

'That's Earth is it? Can't say I like it much. Too hot and the gravity is a drag,' said Kevin.

Simone's voice was full of wonder. 'How fast does this thing move?'

'It took less than a second to get from the land of the boxes to here,' said Kevin.

'And we don't even know where that was,' said Simone. 'I had assumed it was somewhere on Mars and the Box had moved while we were asleep.'

Kevin looked around at the interior of the Box. A table and chairs, sofa, a video screen, and a door to an adjoining bathroom. It didn't look like the the interior of an incredibly fast spaceship. To be fair, the outside didn't look like it could move at all, let alone faster than the speed of light.

Simone, who had joined him in quiet contemplation, broke the silence. 'I was making sure my thoughts were about home for humans, not whatever alien's built that other place.'

'I guess that puts us in Africa somewhere,' said Kevin.

'Hang on.' Simone straightened and lifted her head so she was looking slightly above his head. He had noticed she had started to do this when talking to the Box. 'Box, show a local topographic map.'

The screen view changed from the cliff face to a top down map. There was a gently pulsing small blue square in the middle of the display. Kevin assumed this represented the Box. There was what appeared to be buildings near their position.

'We should investigate those.' Simone pointed at the buildings.

'How far is it? There's no scale.'

'Box, display scale in kilometres.'

As requested, a scale was displayed on the left hand side of the map in kilometres.

'How does this thing know what a kilometre is?' asked Kevin.

'It's an alien mind reading machine, remember?'

'Right. Magic,' said Kevin. He looked at the map again. 'It looks like it's only a kilometre to the first structures. Look, there's a road we can use.'

'I'm not sure I'll be able to walk that far in that gravity,' said Simone.

'You're right.' Kevin had an idea. 'Box, fabricate two assist exoskeletons.'

There was a hum, and the door of the creation compartment slid open. Kevin reached in and pulled out a flat-pack box. A label read 'Rewalk Assist Exoskeleton'.

'How come the damn things got a brand name?' asked Kevin.

'They're the only ones I know of.' Simone shrugged.

Kevin ripped open the packaging to reveal a set of sleek black plastic shrouded assist servos, fitted with nylon straps. There was one for each limb and a larger set for the back and neck, all designed to aid atrophied muscles. 'Nice. These look like top of the range models,' said Kevin.

'It's a good job I was working in the hospital during the collapse of mine sector three,' said Simone.

'That's right. Old Randall got fitted out with one of these.' Kevin was trying to strap one of the servos onto his leg.

'Wait. Let me.' Simone took the servo from him and turned it the right way up.

'Thanks,' said Kevin.

'They really should have put a "This Way Up" label on these,' said Simone as she adjusted the straps to fit snugly.

Kevin offered his other leg to Simone, and she strapped on the second leg servo.

'Maybe we can get some spare parts for the dig-units,' said Kevin.

'Really? We're here, on another world, and all you can think about is getting some spares?'

Kevin raised his hands. 'Alright, we can do the tourist bit as well. But we haven't had any supplies from Earth for years. Let's not ignore an opportunity.'

Simone grabbed one of his raised hands and started to attach another black servo to his arm. 'But it looks like we can make anything we need with the Box.'

'For the whole colony? Are you sure about that?' Kevin flexed his arm. There was a quiet whine as the servos assisted his movement.

'I suppose,' said Simone as she tightened the last strap on

his other arm and started on the larger back and neck support.

Kevin watched his sister shed her excitement and shift into what he thought of as her 'full-on analytical science mode'.

'The full fabrication capabilities of the Box are still an unknown,' said Simone. 'There may well be limitations on quantity.'

'Yeah. That,' said Kevin. He stood up, accompanied by the whir of servo assistance. 'This feels really weird, you should try it.'

'I will. If you'll help me fit mine.'

Kevin whirred his way to the creation unit and retrieved the second package. Simone deftly fitted the servos to her legs. The arm units took a little longer as she needed Kevin's help and he was still getting used to the servo assist reducing the effort needed to move. By the time they had finished he had managed to get a modicum of control over his limbs.

'Almost ready,' said Simone. 'Box, two hats please. Make them green.'

'So, we're going to get some stuff for the colony?' asked Kevin.

'Yes, you're right. We should take the time to load up on supplies if we can. But first' – Simone grinned at him and held out one of the newly fabricated green wide-brimmed hats – 'we do some sightseeing.'

'Agreed.' Kevin took the proffered hat and put it on his head. 'Now, can you get the Box to make me a t-shirt that says "I'm with stupid"?'

CHAPTER 12

Daniel was beginning to wonder if they'd forgotten about him when the pol-AI's voice came from a speaker grille fitted above the door. 'The prisoner will stand behind the yellow line.'

So that's what the yellow line was for. Daniel obstinately remained lying down on the bed.

'The prisoner will stand behind the yellow line,' repeated the AI.

Daniel continued to ignore it. He wondered if it would give up?

'If the prisoner does not stand behind the yellow line, pacification measures will be taken.'

Pacification measures? Daniel didn't think they sounded like much fun. With a protesting click from his knees, he stood up and shuffled behind the yellow line. He glared at the speaker grille, daring it to say something. However, it seemed his compliance with the AI's request was satisfactory and the door unlocked with a loud clunk and swung open to reveal a tall ColPol officer writing something on a clipboard.

'Ah, Daniel Maddock. If you'll come this way.' The

man stepped to one side and gestured for Daniel to leave the cell.

Daniel did as he was told and was taken back through the station to the entry desk.

'You'll be glad to know, you are being released.'

Daniel just nodded. He still wasn't sure what was going on.

'You will make sure you are wearing your cuff at all times. This is a condition of your release.'

Daniel looked at his wrist. The cuff's display had a small blue ColPol icon in the corner.

'If the cuff goes off-net or has been removed for longer than thirty minutes a ColPol team will be despatched to arrest you.'

They were treating him like a common criminal who was deemed safe to release but who they wanted to keep tabs on.

The ColPol officer continued with his monologue. 'Any attempt to enter a restricted area will result in a ColPol team being despatched to arrest you.'

'Restricted area?' asked Daniel.

'Your cuff will alert you when you are near one.' The officers tone was bored. Daniel supposed he'd gone over this many times before.

'Oh, right.' Daniel eyed his cuff suspiciously.

'Now, if you'll just give me your thumbprint here.'

A small beige box with a thumb sized glass panel was presented to Daniel. He pressed his thumb on the glass until the box beeped. The officer took the box back and pushed a black plastic tray across the desk which contained his therms, tank-belt and mask. Daniel took the items from the tray.

'And you're free to go. The main airlock is just behind you.'

Daniel was still in a daze when he left the ColPol building. He was standing outside gathering his thoughts when the airlock opened again and a man exited. Daniel recognised the worn therms with the green cloth patch of an agri-dome worker on one shoulder. Dimitri was swearing loudly and offering various opinions on the ancestry of the ColPol officers.

'Hello, Dimitri,' said Daniel.

'Danny. So, they let you out too. Did they program your cuff with that tracker bullshit?'

'Yes, I think so. They said something about restricted areas.'

'Hah. They'll know everywhere you go.' Dimitri turned towards the grim concrete ColPol building and shouted, 'Fascists!' The shout came out loud but distorted from his mask's speaker.

Daniel saw a plume of dust on the road moving towards them, and it wasn't long before he could hear the familiar whine of an approaching rover. It stopped nearby, throwing up a plume of dust and small stones as the driver braked hard, slewing the rover around so the door faced them. The door popped open.

'Come. We'll go drink and talk about it.' Dimitri stomped over to the rover and climbed in.

Daniel didn't relish the long walk back to his hab, so he followed Dimitri into the rover.

'They got you as well? What dumb scheme did my useless husband rope you into?' asked the driver. Daniel realised the driver was Lula, Dimitri's long suffering wife.

'This time, my sweet, it was not me,' said Dimitri.

'There's a first time for everything I suppose,' said Lula. She turned the rover in the direction of the communal habs and gunned the electric motor, sending the rover on its way with a gratuitous wheel spin.

Dimitri grabbed at a handrail as the rover bounced over an uneven bit of road. 'So, Danny. What's going on with Kev?'

'Have you not seen the news feed?' asked Daniel.

'No. I came off shift and was picked up by ColPol,' said Dimitri. 'They were asking if Kevin had told me anything about his plans for the artefact and if I was in on the plan.'

'They think Kevin and Simone stole it. What did you tell them?' asked Daniel.

'Everything I knew. Which is nothing.'

'And they held you overnight?' asked Lula. 'What are you not telling me?'

'I told them that if I did know the plan I wouldn't tell that bunch of fascist pricks, so they put me in a cell for a few hours.'

'Oh, Dimitri.' Lula shook her head. 'And you Daniel? Did you call them pricks?'

'No. They just didn't believe me.'

'But they let you both go,' said Lula.

'Come to think of it, it does seem strange,' said Daniel.

'They expect us to be in contact with the daring thieves,' said Dimitri.

'I was there when it vanished,' said Daniel. 'It was after they zapped it with a ray gun.'

'A ray gun? What is this, Flash Gordon?' Dimitri laughed.

'The scientist mentioned quantum. It was sort of like a

laser,' said Daniel, straining to remember what he had been told.

'Does it matter?' asked Lula.

'No, I suppose it doesn't,' said Daniel.

'I don't know about you Danny, but I could use a drink,' said Dimitri.

'I guess so,' said Daniel. He wouldn't normally touch alcohol this early in the day but this was not a normal day.

'Lula, my darling, take us to dome six.'

Lula nodded and drove past the communal habs and on towards the gleaming glass of the agri-domes.

Once they had arrived at agri-dome number six, Dimitri led them through a small maintenance airlock and into the bowels of the water storage area. The way was dimly lit, the flicker of a defective light giving the place a run down and neglected feel.

'Goddamn lights. Maintenance apparently don't have enough spares for places no-one visits,' said Dimitri.

It was the same all across the colony. It had been years since the last spacecraft had come from Earth, and the colony was starting to fall apart.

After ten minutes of negotiating the cramped walkways, surrounded by pipes and tubes, they arrived at their destination. There, nestled amongst the legitimate piping and water tanks, was a still. It was cobbled together with vessels and pipes purloined from agri-dome supplies and was bubbling quietly to itself. Not far from the still was a large plastic vat, wedged into a gap in the pipes covering the wall. Daniel assumed that this was the source of the faint, yeasty, sweet smell that was in the air. A small foldable table and some chairs had been deployed within reach of the still; a battered deck of cards was spread out on the table in a half-finished game of solitaire. An old laboratory fridge next to the table hummed quietly to itself.

'Welcome to the distillery. Sit.' Dimitri gestured towards the table and chairs.

Daniel sat down. Lula took the seat opposite him and swept the cards from the table and started to shuffle them. Dimitri placed three small measuring cylinders on the table and squirted a 50ml measure of clear liquid into each of them from a bottle misleadingly labelled 'distilled water'.

Daniel picked up a cylinder and sniffed it. He couldn't smell much. Maybe the merest hint of apple.

'Drink up, Danny.' Dimitri tossed back his drink in one smooth motion.

Daniel followed suit and exploded into a gasping cough as the drink burned its way down his oesophagus.

Dimitri laughed and banged the table with the flat of his palm.

'Macho bullshit.' Lula pushed the measuring cylinder in front her towards her husband. 'Put some juice in mine.'

Dimitri, tears of laughter in his eyes, retrieved a white plastic carton from the fridge.

'I'm sorry Danny, just my little joke.' He poured a golden liquid from the carton into Lula's cylinder. The smell of fresh apple juice floated across the table. He then fixed himself and Daniel another drink. This time with an apple juice mixer.

'So, what do we think has happened to Kev?' asked Dimitri.

'And Simone,' said Lula.

Dimitri nodded. 'Yes, and Simone.'

'I don't know. ColPol seem to think they had some big plan to steal the artefact. But I just don't see it.'

'You're right. Your boy Kev does not have the balls for something as big as that.' Dimitri poured himself another drink. 'So, your boy is gone—'

'And girl,' Lula interjected.

'Yes, yes. Boy and girl. Both gone. Question is Danny, what are we going to do about it?'

'Do?' Daniel was genuinely puzzled. 'There's nothing we can do, is there?'

'I tell you' – Dimitri leaned forward, his voice dropping to a low whisper – 'what we do is go and see for ourselves what is going on at this "dig site"'.

'I told you, I was there. I saw it disappear,' said Daniel.

'You saw what they wanted you to see,' declared Dimitri. He leant back on his chair and drained his measuring cylinder before banging it down on the table. 'We'll go there and find out for ourselves.'

'Hang on. You said earlier that ColPol let us go in the hope Kevin and Simone would contact us.'

'Yes. So?'

Daniel was having trouble following the tortured logic of Dimitri's thinking. 'But why would they be doing that if what I saw happen didn't actually happen?'

'Those ColPol pricks don't know what's going on. This smells like a council cover up to me,' said Dimitri firmly. His voice was filled with righteous conviction.

'I don't know. It seems like nobody knows what really happened.'

'See? One big cover up. We will go and find out for ourselves what is going on.'

Lula had a resigned smile on her face. 'I find it easier just to let him do what he wants when he's like this.'

Dimitri pointed a finger at his wife. 'You know I am right.' He looked at his cuff. 'First, we need to fix our cuffs.'

'Right. The restricted area protocol,' said Daniel. 'How are you going to do that?'

'Don't worry about that Danny. I know a guy.'

'Idiot,' said Lula. 'I can take care of that.' She waggled her fingers.

'How?' asked Daniel.

'Of course, my beloved husband wouldn't bother to tell you what I do. I'm an AI engineer. I'll just move my fingers across the keyboard and make it happen.'

'Best in the business,' said Dimitri proudly.

'That may be a slight exaggeration, but working around the ColPol alerts will be no problem.'

'And they won't find out?' asked Daniel. He didn't want any more trouble than he was already in.

'Nope. As soon as someone accesses that node, my code will self-delete.'

Dimitri clapped Daniel on the back. 'Then we are agreed, yes? First, Lula fixes our cuffs. Then we uncover the truth.'

CHAPTER 13

A rusted, weatherbeaten sign had announced the name of the settlement as 'Akpoort'. By the side of the road, Kevin and Simone passed some long abandoned vehicles, vegetation sprouting from them like an avant garde garden decoration. The first building they came across was a church. The once white paint was peeling from the wooden walls and its large windows were all broken. Graves marked with crude crosses overran the surrounding graveyard boundary, radiating out from the church in a haphazard explosion of bereavement. Everything was still, the silence only broken by the faint whirring of their assist servos.

Simone suddenly stopped. 'Oh, Kevin. Look!' Simone was pointing at one of the nearby grave markers. A brown bird with a yellow backside, its talons clutching the top of the cross, was regarding them. Its head made short, sharp movements as it appraised them from different angles.

Kevin watched the bird, fascinated. He had, of course, seen birds before on screen. But never in real life.

'It's beautiful,' said Simone.

He thought this was probably overstating it a little bit.

This was, however, the first sign of life they had seen. 'Sim.'

'Yes?'

'Does this all seem a bit' – he swept his arm around in a wide arc, taking in the bird the graves and the church – 'post-apocalyptic to you?'

'Maybe. A little. Let's see what it's like in town.'

Within five minutes of reaching the town, Kevin had decided it also looked decidedly post-apocalyptic. Massive heaps of rubble lined the street, barely recognisable as the remains of buildings. The few buildings that remained intact stood a lonely vigil over their fallen comrades. The street itself was deserted, the only vehicles a few abandoned cars at the side of the road. They came across a truck in a ditch, its loading doors open and contents long gone. Kevin climbed into the cab to find it also empty, a pair of sad green dice hanging above the dashboard. They left the truck behind as they moved closer to the centre of town.

'This is beginning to creep me out,' said Kevin.

'I know what you mean. Everything I've read or seen about Earth said how overcrowded it was.'

'And there's no bugger here,' said Kevin.

'There's got to be someone. We just have to keep looking,' said Simone.

Kevin cupped his hands around his mouth, threw his head back and shouted, 'Hello, is anybody there?'

His voice echoed around the empty streets before fading into silence. They both stood still and listened. There was an explosion of wings as a dark, black shape took off from a nearby roof and scudded low across the road in front of them. Kevin jumped back, his servos whining in response to his rapid muscle contractions.

'Another bird,' said Simone.

'I knew that.' Kevin stood up straight. 'Just a little overreaction by the assist servos, that's all.'

Simone smirked. 'Right.'

Suddenly, there was a loud crack and a cloud of dirt puffed into the air a couple of metres in front of them. The sharp retort echoed off the ruined buildings.

Kevin jumped back, his servos apparently malfunctioning again. 'What the hell?'

Simone had dropped to a crouch and was scanning the windows on those buildings that were not completely collapsed.

'Stay where you are, don't move.' A woman's voice. It was hard to tell where it was coming from. Somewhere in front of them was as good a fix as Kevin could get. He recognised the accent as South African from some of the old Science Fiction films he'd watched with his dad.

He whispered, 'That was probably a gunshot.' Again, he recognised that noise from the world of film. There were no guns on Mars. Using them in a pressurised colony building would be dangerous for the shooter as well as the target. In the early days of the colony, before fabrication facilities that had the capability to manufacture firearms were available, they were possibly the last thing that anyone would pay to ship from Earth. Once the fab-units were up and running, nobody bothered. What would you shoot at on Mars anyway? Apart from each other that is. Nobody wanted some Martian cracking under the day-to-day hardships of colonial life and taking it out on the other members of his (or her) communal hab.

'A gunshot?' asked Simone.

She seemed to be having trouble getting to grips with the concept, so Kevin stepped forwards, trying to interpose his body between his sister and whoever had them in their sights. 'We don't mean any harm.' Kevin raised his hands, empty and palms forward.

'Put your tech on the ground and put your hands on your head,' instructed the hidden gunwoman.

'What?' asked Kevin.

'She means our servos and cuffs,' whispered Simone.

Kevin kept his voice low. 'We'll never make it back without the assist servos.'

'Stop whispering to each other. I can see you doing it.'

Kevin thought the voice was coming from a building that was relatively intact about twenty metres ahead of them. A sign above the door and large broken window read 'KFC' in red on what probably used to be a white background. It was so encrusted with dirt it was hard to tell. There was a stylised picture of a smiling bespectacled gentleman next to the letters.

'Where is everyone?' asked Kevin.

'Stop playing dumb and drop the tech.'

'But we won't be able to get back without it,' said Simone.

There was a moments silence. 'What are those boxes strapped to you anyway?'

'Servo assist units. They give us the help we need to walk here,' said Simone.

'You two cripples?'

'No,' said Kevin. Kevin wished his sister hadn't announced the fact they couldn't walk easily unassisted.

'Why do you need help walking? You sick?' This time, the woman's voice was tinged with a genuine note of fear.

'We're not sick,' said Kevin. He didn't see much point in being coy about where they were from. 'We're from Mars.'

'Mars?'

'The red planet. Fourth rock from the sun. You know, Mars,' said Kevin.

'Less of the bullshit. Who are you?'

'It's the truth. We just got here. Wherever here is,' said Kevin.

A figure stepped out from the cover of a doorway. She wore khaki fatigues and had a rifle levelled at them. 'You're in Akpoort, or what's left of it.'

'Hi, I'm Kevin.' Kev gave a little wave which was accompanied by the whirr of his servos.

'And I'm Simone.'

'She's my sister,' said Kevin.

'Kevin and Simone, I am asking nicely. Put your tech on the ground.'

'But I told you, we need it,' said Simone.

'If what you've told me is true, then you'll be easier to handle without it.'

'What do you mean, easier to handle?' asked Kevin.

'No more talking. Do it.' The gun was waved menacingly in their direction.

Kevin didn't like it, but it looked like they had no choice. First he took off his cuff and tossed it to the ground, then he sat down in the dirt and started to take off his leg assist servo units.

'You too.' The gun was moved so it pointed squarely at Simone.

By now Kevin had removed the leg servos and was struggling with the straps holding the unit on his right arm. 'Give me a hand Sim.'

Simone, who had been hesitating, got to her knees and helped him remove the assist servos. Then, Kevin helped her do the same.

'Now stand up.' The business end of the rifle was waved to emphasise the request.

Kevin put his hands beneath him and laboriously heaved himself to his feet. Working unaided against the full force of Earth's gravity was distinctly unpleasant. It was nearly three times as strong as Mars gravity, making his limbs feel like they were made of lead. He had to help Simone to her feet; she grimaced and let out a small grunt as she stood up.

'Now over there,' instructed the woman. She pointed at the centre of the road.

Kevin, half supporting his sister, shuffled towards the indicated spot.

The woman moved to the pile of tech, slung her rifle over her shoulder and, with one eye on her captives, picked up one of the servo assist units.

Kevin just watched her, his shoulders stooped under his own body weight.

'These are plastic.' The woman's voice was half accusing, half full of wonder.

'Uh, yes,' said Simone. 'I wasn't thinking of the expensive carbon fibre units.'

'What anti-bacs are you using? I can't feel any residue.'

'Anti-bacs? What?' Simone sat down. Kevin could actually see the strength leaving her as she struggled against the fierce pull of Earth's gravity.

'No anti-bacs?' The woman looked shocked and dropped the unit. Then, she pulled a small glass bottle of clear liquid from a pocket. The top was fitted with a metal pump and she sprayed the servos liberally, making sure she coated every plastic surface. The woman thoughtfully looked from the pile of assist servos to the pitiful state of her captives.'You two might really be from Mars. Put these back on. You're coming with me.'

CHAPTER 14

Daniel wondered how he had ended up here, sneaking into sector seven of the water mine. Sneaking was maybe overstating it. Dimitri had loudly announced their presence to the miner working the night shift in the extraction plant. Bannon had seemed to know the agri-dome worker and let them through, taking a bottle of Dimitri's hooch in exchange. Now, the three of them were walking down the dimly lit access tunnel to where the artefact used to be. According to Bannon, the scientists had all gone home leaving cameras watching for the possible return of the disappearing giant grey cube.

'What about the cameras?' asked Daniel.

'Don't worry about that. They'll see what I want them to see,' said Lula.

She was carrying her ruggedised laptop. Daniel assumed she would work some programmer magic on the digital cameras.

'Here we are,' said Dimitri.

Daniel almost didn't recognise the cavern now that it had been emptied of most of the technical equipment and the multitude of scientists who had been here during his last visit. The hole that used to contain the enigmatic grey cube was floodlit and had multiple cameras trained on it. From this vantage point, the void left by the departed artefact looked cavernously large.

'Hah, all the cameras are watching that hole,' said Dimitri.

Daniel realised he was right, all the tripod-mounted cameras were pointing in the same direction, leaving them free to poke around the rest of the cavern undetected.

'Saves me a job,' observed Lula.

'But here is another one for you,' said Dimitri. He was pointing at a piece of computer equipment on a steel work-bench. Daniel had no idea what it was for, but it was powered, the winking of green LEDs showing the flow of data to and from the unit.

Lula scooped up a chair that was lying on its side, forgotten during the exodus. She plopped it down in front of the workbench, sat on it, then opened her laptop and plugged it into the mystery bit of equipment.

'Let's see what you have to tell us.' Lula's fingers were a blur over the keyboard as she did something that, as far as Daniel was concerned, was bordering on techno-magic.

Dimitri was poking about a small pile of detritus. Daniel went over to join him.

'Best stay out of the way, eh Danny?'

'Your wife is very talented,' said Daniel.

'Don't let her hear you say that. Her goddamn head is big enough already.'

Daniel picked up a discarded black folder. It was empty.

'There's nothing here Danny.' Dimitri kicked the pile of rubbish in disgust.

'Let's hope Lula has more luck.'

Dimitri nodded and strode over to his wife's side. 'Any luck my little love muffin?'

'Sort of,' said Lula. She did not look up from the screen.

'Do you care to explain to your somewhat simple husband?'

'There's no information here,' started Lula.

'Crap,' said Dimitri.

'Before you turn the air blue, I haven't finished.'

'Sorry.' Dimitri shuffled his feet reminding Daniel of a chastised child. A six foot chastised child.

'I have inserted my code to spoof the camera inputs and monitoring programs to transmit any alerts to my cuff instead of their control application.'

Dimitri clapped his hands and kissed the top of his wife's head. 'Good! I knew there was a reason I married you.'

Lula tilted her head back to look him in the eye. 'Just one?'

'One of many, one of many.' Dimitri spun on his heel. 'Come, Danny. Time for us to go.'

Lula snapped her laptop shut and stood up. The three of them then retraced their steps and, waving to Bannon on their way through the extraction plant, made their way back out of the mine to the surface.

CHAPTER 15

Kevin and Simone walked further into town. Connie was taking no chances, keeping them in front of her at all times. She had finally decided to introduce herself while they were strapping on their assist servos. Kevin had been trying to guess her age. Her features were weathered, but the post-apocalyptic vibe Kevin was getting from Akpoort suggested that life was hard, and Kevin had indecisively settled on 'somewhere between 30 and 50'.

Connie took them down deserted streets until they arrived at what looked like the town's hospital. Kevin was still getting used to the buildings. They were all so square and covered with non-pressure safe windows and doors. Most of the hospital buildings were as run down and abandoned looking as the rest of the town. Connie herded them towards a building whose windows had been modified around the seals with strips of painted metal fixed over where the glass joined the frames.

The sight of a biohazard sign at the side of the access road made Kevin stop. 'Biohazard?'

'Just keep moving.' The waving gun barrel left him little option.

'What is this place?' asked Simone. There had been a

sign above the door, but it had either fallen off or someone had removed it.

'Home,' said Connie. She strode past the pair and banged on the door. 'Open up, its Connie. I've brought home a couple of strays.'

A stooped old man in a tartan bathrobe opened the door. He had a pair of glasses perched on his nose which he peered over like a disapproving headmaster.

'Strangers, Connie? I don't think Ray will like that.'

'Ray can kiss my black arse,' said Connie.

'Mind your language young lady. What will your guests think?'

Another wave of the gun indicated that Kevin and Simone were to enter. Kevin stepped through first, shooting a nervous smile at the old man, who had backed off to a second door that presumably led into the building proper. Kevin realised the room they were stood in reminded him of the airlocks back home.

'Ok, strip,' said Connie.

Kevin looked at her in surprise. 'What?'

Connie had rested her rifle against a wall and was undoing the metal buttons on her khaki jacket. 'And Charlie? You can go now.'

The old man, Charlie, muttering to himself, turned and left via the internal door.

'Your clothes, put them in the basket.' Connie pointed at a large wire basket.

'Why?' asked Kevin.

'Because I said so.'

Kevin hesitated.

'And they need to be sterilised.'

Kevin looked at her. His expression must have accurately conveyed his lack of comprehension.

'Got to make sure we don't carry any polly inside,' said Connie.

'Any what?' asked Simone.

'Polimero ethanolica.'

'Is that some sort of bacteria? That doesn't particularly help,' said Simone.

'The goddamn plastic eating superbug.' Connie shook her head and peeled off her trousers. 'Strip off. Now.'

Kevin and Simone proceeded to remove their assist servos and clothes under the watchful eye of a now naked, gun-toting Connie. Kevin revised his age estimate downwards in light of new facts revealed. He was glad the danger, oppressive gravity, and general weirdness of the situation was suppressing any natural reaction he might have had to the sight of Connie.

Once they had finished, Kevin awkwardly covered his modesty with both hands (not that he needed both), and Connie opened the interior door. This led to a second room which was tiled and fitted with chrome shower units.

'In you go.' Connie pushed Kevin's shoulder, propelling him towards the open doorway.

Kevin took the hint and stepped over the threshold and stood under one of the showerheads. He studiously averted his gaze from his sister and Connie as they followed him, instead focusing on the tarnished chrome shower fittings above his head. He shut his eyes as water blasted down onto him. There was a strong disinfectant smell to the water, and he guessed this was to make sure any stray bacteria on his skin was definitely dealt with. This, he felt, was a good thing. A plastic eating superbug sounded bad.

After their awkward group shower, Connie herded them into a third room containing steel lockers. She gave them a blue hospital gown each. Kevin noticed that she had left the rifle leant against a locker, and he hoped she had stopped viewing them as a threat.

'Sorry,' said Connie as she pulled on a pair of faded blue jeans; a view that Kevin found distracting. 'Your stuff is being washed.'

'Thankyou, Connie,' said Simone.

Kevin donned his gown facing into a corner of the room, counted to thirty, and then turned around. He was relieved to see that the two women had finished dressing. A glance at his sister's face told him she was struggling with the gravity as much as he was.

Simone fixed Connie with her tired gaze. 'Connie, I need to sit down.'

'So you say. Well, you'll be able to rest while Ray talks to you.' Connie opened the next door and stepped through. She still held the rifle loosely in her right hand.

Kevin offered his arm to Simone, who gratefully took it, leaning on her brother.

Connie poked her head back through the door. 'Come on.'

* * *

Kevin sagged into the chair, his arms hanging heavily into his lap. Next to him, Simone was leaning forward, elbows on her knees and her head cradled in her hands. A middle-aged man, he had introduced himself simply as 'Ray', was sitting across the desk opposite, regarding them through steepled fingers. They were sitting in a cluttered room filled with paper and filing cabinets. A half empty bottle of whisky perched on the corner of the desk. Kevin reflected that, on Mars, that bottle represented luxury only enjoyed by the most senior council members.

'Would you like a glass?' asked Ray.

'Yes, but it's probably not a good idea. I'm feeling tired enough as it is,' said Kevin.

'Because you're from Mars,' said Ray.

Kevin nodded.

'As in the red planet.'

'That's the one,' said Kevin.

'Forgive me if I find that a little hard to believe,' said Ray.

Kevin couldn't muster the energy to say anything.

'However" – Ray looked at Simone, who was still bent over holding her head – 'either you're good actors, or you are indeed suffering from the effects of being at 1g.'

'Trust me, this isn't an act,' said Kevin.

'In that case, it would be unconscionably rude of me to keep these from you.' Ray gestured at the assist servos which had been stacked neatly on a nearby chair after being thoroughly sterilised. 'Please, go ahead.'

With a sense of relief, Kevin first helped Simone fit her servos, then gratefully accepted her help to don his. They made quite a sorry sight in their hospital gowns and servos, more like decrepit victims of some muscle wasting disease than healthy adults.

'Oh, that's better,' said Kevin. Servos whirred, assisting him as he flexed his arms.

'Remarkable. If what you say is true, I would really like to know how and why you are in Akpoort.'

'It's going to sound crazy,' said Kevin.

Simone kicked Kevin under the desk. He glanced over and saw her shake her head almost imperceptibly. Unfortunately, the sound of her neck assist servo gave the motion away.

Ray's eyes flicked from Kevin to Simone and back again. 'Interesting.'

'Uh,' said Kevin.

'Continue, and please leave nothing out.'

Kevin looked at Simone. She shrugged.

'We, uh, we came in an alien box,' said Kevin. He didn't really know what else to say.

'Excuse me?'

'A box. Made by aliens,' said Kevin. 'It's quite big.'

Ray looked at them in silence for an uncomfortable amount of time before he said, 'This alien box, where is it now?'

'It's not far,' interjected Simone.

'Where exactly?'

'It would be easier to show you,' said Simone.

Ray smiled slightly. 'Very well. You will take us to see this box for ourselves.'

'Of course,' said Simone.

The trip back to the Box was quicker as they took a more direct route. Kevin and Simone were leading the way, a vigilant Connie keeping her rifle at the ready behind them. Ray and two other men were behind Connie and talked together in low voices for much of the trip. They were also armed. Kevin wondered if they'd been lucky not to encounter whatever their hosts were wary of.

'Holy shit,' said Connie as the Box came into view.

'I have to admit, I had my doubts.' Ray slapped Kevin on the back. 'But it is as impressive as you described.'

Ray walked past them and walked a circuit of the Box, ending up back where he started in front of Kevin and Simone. 'How do we get in?'

'Only I can open it.'

Ray nodded slowly. 'Very well. You will go inside with Connie.'

'Ok,' said Simone.

She moved towards the box and Kevin started to follow.

'Not you,' said Ray, putting a hand on Kevin's shoulder.

Simone stopped looked over her shoulder at Kevin. He nodded at her. He'd be alright.

She turned back to face the Box. 'Box, open the door.'

The circular opening popped into existence.

Connie took a step back, raising her rifle.

Simone stepped inside and disappeared from Kevin's view. Connie hesitantly followed, and the opening closed behind her as suddenly as it had appeared.

Ray's grip tightened on Kevin's shoulder. 'I hope for your sake that she isn't going to do anything stupid.'

So do I, thought Kevin. So do I.

Five tense minutes later, Simone and Connie exited the Box.

'Well?' said Ray.

'It's amazing Ray,' said Connie. 'They're on the level.'

Ray was smiling. It looked decidedly disconcerting to Kevin.

'We will come back tomorrow, and the lovely Simone can show us how it works.'

CHAPTER 16

Lula hooked a chair out from under the table, sat down and opened her laptop.

'Drink, Danny?' asked Dimitri. He had pulled another drink carton from beside the still.

Daniel shook his head and sat down. 'So, what now?'

Dimitri shrugged and joined them at the table. He took a slug from the carton.

Lula softly shook her head and shifted her attention to her computer's screen. Daniel watched as her fingers flew over the keyboard in a blur, the light tapping of the keys overlaying the background noise of the softly gurgling water pipes.

'What are you doing now?' he asked.

'As much as sitting around and drinking appeals' – she shot her husband a sharp look – 'I thought I'd see what is going on with your daughters husband.'

Daniel frowned. 'Jacob?'

'You said he'd been picked up by ColPol,' said Lula.

'Yes, with me.'

'About the same time as Dimitri, right?'

'I guess so,' said Daniel.

'Aren't you wondering why they didn't let him go? And more importantly, what they are doing with him?'

'Oh.' Daniel felt a wave of guilt as he realised he hadn't been thinking about his son-in-law at all.

Lula spun her laptop around. It was displaying a ColPol status screen for Jacob Aarons. Under his picture were the words: 'In Custody' and there was a red 'none' next to release date.

Daniel did not like the look of that. 'None?'

'I guess they've decided to hang on to him for a bit.' Lula spun the laptop around to face her and resumed typing. 'I'll try and find out some more.'

'They can't just hold someone like that can they?'

Lula peered at the screen. 'Apparently they can if the prisoner is suspected of "willfully endangering the safety of the colony".'

'What bullshit is that?' asked Dimitri.

'It allows indefinite emergency detention,' said Lula.

'Can't you do anything?' asked Daniel.

Lula shook her head. 'These detention instructions have come from a council AI. If I tamper with them, they'll know.'

'Well, shit,' said Dimitri.

'So we can't help him?' asked Daniel.

'Unless you want to take on a hab full of ColPol and bust him out, no.'

'Not even I think that's a good idea,' said Dimitri.

'For once, my husband is the voice of reason. However...' Lula began to type furiously, sustaining a smooth flow of keystrokes before ending with a flourish on the return key.

'There. I've set up a monitor. I'll get an alert if his status changes,' said Lula.

'Better than nothing,' said Dimitri.

'I've just inserted a bit of code under the electronic noses of the ColPol AIs and all you can say is "Better than nothing"?'

Dimitri held his hands up. 'Sorry! Sorry. What I meant to say was: thank you, my most talented wife. I do not deserve you.' His smile was mischievous.

'For that, you can go and find us some dinner.'

Dimitri kept his hands raised in surrender as he stood up. 'Fine. I'll go raid the dome, I'll be back soon.'

Daniel watched Dimitri's retreating back before turning to find Lula watching him over the top of her laptop. He felt bad about forgetting Jacob and even though they couldn't help him at the moment, he was glad that Lula had managed to do something.

'So, Daniel,' began Lula. 'Or do you prefer Danny?'

'I prefer Daniel actually. It's only Dimitri who calls me Danny.'

'Typical.' Lula snorted a short laugh. 'Anyway. Jacob's rap sheet reads like a great work of fiction. Unauthorised gene-editing, conspiracy to appropriate colony property and, not forgetting, endangering the safety of the colony.'

'This whole situation is crazy,' said Daniel.

'I've only met Jacob a couple of times, but he doesn't strike me as someone to rock the colonial boat. Unlike my idiot husband.'

'He isn't. At least he wasn't.'

'Explain?'

'The council. They've been blocking human trials of gene-editing and cutting the funding of the Program.'

'I remember it was being pushed as the way forward a few years ago,' said Lula.

'Yes, before Doris—'. Daniel lapsed into silence.

'Sorry, Daniel.' Lula leant forwards and put a hand on his shoulder.

Daniel nodded. He could feel his eyes beginning to prick with tears. 'That's alright.' He heard his own voice, trembling and thick with emotion. 'God, it's stupid. Getting like this when I try and talk about—'. He stopped again.

Lula stood and walked around the table. She stood behind him and wordlessly wrapped her arms around him.

Daniel broke; he leant his head on Lula's arm and sobbed, all the feelings from the day of the accident surging back over him in a crashing wave.

'Hey. Let it out,' said Lula.

Daniel sniffed and lifted his head. 'Thanks. I'm sorry.'

'Don't be. I can't imagine losing Dimitri like that.'

'It just seems so unfair. Do you know how unlikely a multiple tank failure is on a belt?'

'Was that what it was?' asked Lula.

'That's what they told me. Imagining her final moments, running out of air—'

Daniel could feel the sobs coming back and stopped talking. He felt Lula's arms move away and opened his eyes to see her move back to sit behind her laptop and start typing, an intense look on her face.

He sniffed. 'What are you doing?'

'Checking the ColPol records on the accident.'

'What?'

'And – that's strange.'

'What?' asked Daniel, again.

'The text on file does describe a tank failure and the dates check out, but the embedded timestamps are wrong.'

'What?' Daniel couldn't help noticing he was repeating himself.

'The report has been modified since it was first logged.'

'What are you saying?' asked Daniel. 'I don't understand.'

'Someone has changed the content of this report.'

'So, they added some extra detail or fixed some spelling?'

'More pervasive than that. A superficial inspection of the report wouldn't see anything wrong.' Lula peered over the top of her laptop at Daniel. 'But I don't do superficial inspection.'

'So, what's different?' asked Daniel.

'Pretty much all of it after the initial incident report.'

'What did it say before?'

Lula's fingers flew over the keyboard in another burst of typing. 'Damn it.'

'What?' Daniel figured he might as well go all in with his new catchphrase.

Lula leaned back in her chair and wiped her face with her hands. 'Nothing. I can only tell what's new, not what was there before.'

'What do they have to hide?' asked Daniel.

'No idea. I also wonder who "they" are,' said Lula.

'Can you find anything more out?'

'Maybe. I'm going to need to get admin access to one of the ColPol AI's to do it.'

Dimitri chose this point to make a reappearance. He was carrying a box marked with the green tree logo of the agri-domes. Lula hurriedly moved her laptop out of the way as

Dimitri banged the box onto the table and flipped open the lid.

'To do what?' asked Dimitri.

Lula caught the apple that Dimitri tossed at her. 'Find out what's been faked and by who, in the report on Doris's accident.'

'Lula has found evidence of the report being tampered with,' said Daniel.

'A conspiracy,' said Dimitri.

'Obviously,' agreed Lula. 'And I aim to find out who is behind it.'

'Of course. I would expect nothing else.' Dimitri took a large crunching bite out of his apple and chewed.

'Thankyou,' said Daniel. The possibility of Doris's death not being an accident was just starting to sink in. He felt a small kernel of anger, which had been directed at the universe in general when his wife died, sharpen and acquire a new focus. If someone had killed her, they would pay. He would make sure of it.

CHAPTER 17

Kevin was woken by a loud banging on the door to their room. Yesterday, they had been shown to what looked like a hospital room with two beds. Any illusions they had harboured about any freedom they would be allowed was dispelled when the door had been locked behind them. Kevin did not remember much after that having slipped into an exhausted slumber almost as soon as his head hit the pillow.

The door opened and Connie stepped inside. 'Rise and shine. Eat some breakfast then it's time to go.' She lobbed something onto each of the beds, then left the room, locking the door behind her.

Kevin sat up and picked up what appeared to be some sort of large biscuit. He peeled back the paper wrapper and bit into it. It had a cardboard like texture and a bland taste.

'Yuck,' said Simone.

Kevin swallowed his mouthful of bland breakfast before responding. 'I agree, and there I was thinking food would be better on Earth.'

'I was expecting more people,' said Simone.

Sometime during the night, their clothes had been disinfected and left in a neatly folded pile on a chair. They had finished their breakfast and Kevin was putting on his boots when the door opened to admit Connie. She was carrying her rifle.

Connie nodded her head towards Simone. 'Alright, on your feet, time to go.' Her rifle swung round to point at Kevin. 'Not you. You're to stay here as a guarantee of Simone's good behaviour.'

'I don't want to go anywhere without my brother,' said Simone.

'Ray's orders. I'm sorry, you don't get the choice,' said Connie.

Kevin looked nervously at the barrel of the gun. 'Go on Sim. I'm sure it will be alright.'

'Like hell I will,' said Simone.

'You should listen to your brother,' said Connie.

Simone visibly hesitated, her gaze shifting from Kevin to the gun-toting Connie and back again.

Kevin nodded at her and tried to smile reassuringly. 'I'll stay here and sample some more of the fine cuisine.' He held up the empty biscuit wrapper.

This drew a laugh from Connie. 'See? He'll be fine.'

Simone still looked unsure.

'You go on and take them to the Box. You can come back for me later.' He saw Connie's attention shift to see Simone's response and quickly winked at his sister in what he hoped was a meaningful fashion.

'Right. Yes. I guess I can.' Simone slowly nodded as she said this.

'Great. Can we go now? Ray isn't known for his patience,' said Connie.

Once Simone and Connie had gone Kevin sighed and sank back onto the bed, letting the springs take the weight of his body. He wondered if he would ever get used to the gravity here. His muscles would strengthen over time, but he didn't intend on staying here that long. Kevin just had to hope that Simone could pull off some Box-based trickery, escape Ray's clutches and come and rescue him.

* * *

Simone was tired. Ray had not allowed her to use her assist servos and the extra weight she now carried was telling. She had led Ray, Connie and three other men, who had not been introduced, back to the Box. It was still where they had left it, looking large and immovable.

'Right, in we go,' said Ray.

Simone nodded wearily. 'Box, open the door.'

A circular opening suddenly appeared in the side of the Box and Simone started towards it.

'Ah, ah. Connie first,' said Ray.

Connie nodded and stepped over the threshold in front of Simone.

'Now you.' Ray waved his revolver at her.

Simone stepped inside and stopped, letting her eyes adjust to the gloom. Connie was standing in front of her, still getting used to the reduced gravity inside the Box.

She heard Ray's voice behind her, 'Move.'

This was it. If she didn't act now, Ray and the others would be with her inside the box.

She moved her lips, silently mouthing the words 'Box, close the door' and launched herself at Connie.

Everything seemed to happen in slow motion as Connie brought the rifle up and Simone crashed into her, knocking the barrel back down towards the floor. The harsh retort of the gun being discharged filled the inside of the Box, then Connie toppled backwards, lost her grip on the gun and had the breath knocked out of her when she took the full force of Simone's fall.

Simone scrambled to her feet. She knew she had to act quickly, she'd never win in a straight fight with the more muscled Earth woman. Connie was still struggling to her feet, the low gravity throwing her balance off, which gave Simone just enough time to get to the rifle first and swing it round to point at her.

Connie stopped in a half crouch and slowly raised her hands. 'Let's not be hasty.'

'Hasty? You're the one who kidnapped us and plans to steal the box.'

'Look, that was Ray.' Connie glanced at the blank featureless wall where the opening to the outside had been. 'And he is probably really pissed about now.'

'So? He can't get in.'

'But he can go back and take it out on your brother,' said Connie.

Simone smiled slyly. 'Not if I get there first.'

'How? There's no way you'll beat him back. I saw how exhausted you were moving around in our gravity.'

'Box, duct tape please.'

The creation compartment opened to reveal a new roll of duct tape.

'Wait, just think about this for a minute,' said Connie.

Simone tossed the tape so it landed by Connie. 'Tape your legs together.'

She kept the gun trained on Connie until she had finished wrapping several winds of tape around her legs.

Then, she put the rifle to one side and taped Connie's hands together.

Simone stepped back to admire her handiwork. 'Now you're secured, time to get Kevin.'

'You'll never get back in time. Ray will be halfway there by now.'

Simone smiled at Connie. 'Box, go to Kevin's prison.'

There was no indication that anything had happened.

'Seriously. Free me and I won't tell Ray,' said Connie. 'He can get mean when he's disobeyed.'

'Box, open the door.'

The circular opening snapped open to reveal a grinning Kevin standing in what appeared to be a pile of rubble. Simone returned her brothers smile.

'Nice entrance,' said Kevin.

'Don't just stand there, come aboard,' said Simone.

Kevin stepped through the opening and stopped, bouncing on his toes. 'God, that's better.'

Simone laughed. 'I know, right?'

The door to the room Kevin had just vacated rattled and was flung open by a man armed with a semi-automatic pistol. Instead of shooting, he stood there his mouth open and a look of pure astonishment on his face.

'Box, close the door!' shouted Simone.

The view of the ruined room and the surprised man disappeared as the wall behind Kevin became blank and featureless.

'Box, go home,' said Simone.

'What just happened?' asked Connie.

'What's she doing here?' asked Kevin, noticing the woman for the first time.

'Trust me, this wasn't my idea,' said Connie.

Kevin spent a moment considering the trussed up woman lying on the floor, then looked at Simone. 'Duct tape?'

Simone shrugged. 'It was that or keep the gun on her all the time.'

'What are we going to do with her now?' asked Kevin.

'I hadn't thought that far ahead,' admitted Simone.

'I suppose we could take her back to Earth and dump her,' said Kevin.

'Hey, I'm right here,' said Connie.

'Maybe,' said Simone.

'Wait. What do you mean "take her back to Earth"?' asked Connie.

Simone looked down at Connie. 'I'm afraid we seem to have perpetrated our own bit of kidnapping.'

Connie lifted her duct taped arms. 'Well, duh.'

'Not just the duct taping. We've physically moved too,' said Simone.

'Moved? Appearing back at the base was pretty amazing,' said Connie.

Simone and Kevin exchanged a glance.

'Why are you looking at each other like that? Where are we now?'

Simone saw Kevin nod at her. Fair enough. No harm in showing Connie the view. 'Box, show outside.'

The flat screen flicked into life showing two rows of giant grey cubes extending into the distance.

Connie struggled to a sitting position. 'Is that what's outside? Where is this place? What are you going to do with me?'

'The answer to your first question is "yes", and the answer to the second two is "I'm not sure",' said Simone.

Connie switched from looking at the image on the screen to the brother and sister. 'Look, I had to do what Ray wanted. It was that or get kicked out of the facility.'

'You were only obeying orders?' asked Kevin.

'Stop it, Kev,' said Simone.

Kevin sat down and put his feet up on the table. 'Come on. She's been the one pointing a gun at us.'

'Like I said. It's do as Ray wants or you get a one-way ticket out of the facility.'

'Would that be so bad?' asked Kevin.

'I can tell you're not from Earth.'

'Is it really that bad? You said something about a plastic eating bacteria.'

'Can I maybe sit on a chair and tell you? This floor is not very comfortable.'

'Oh, sorry,' said Simone. 'Box, another chair please.'

Simone saw Connie's eyes widen as a third chair flowed up from the floor and formed next to the table.

'I'll be damned,' said Connie.

Simone helped Connie into the chair before sitting down herself. She left the duct tape in place.

'You were going to tell us more about Earth. The bacteria,' prompted Simone.

'Polly. It's the damn end of the world, that's what it is.'

'Things did look a little bleak,' said Kevin.

'Bleak? Try gone to shit.'

'What happened?' asked Simone.

'The Children of Gaia.'

'Who?' asked Kevin.

'Bunch of eco-terrorists. Those stupid arseholes released Polly into the sea "to cleanse the oceans".'

'Aren't they all choked with waste plastic? That's a good thing, right?' asked Kevin.

'Sure, until it got a taste for nylon and electrical insulation.'

Simone immediately realised the implications.

Then Connie confirmed them. 'All the cables running under the sea were the first casualties, quickly followed by all the boats.'

'All of them?' asked Simone.

'And then Polly came down in the rain. That's when everything fell apart.'

Simone glanced at Kevin. His face showed a mixture of fascination and horror.

Connie looked grim. 'Then, three years ago, the Armageddon plague hit.'

'Plague? Oh my god,' said Simone.

'Polly got at a secret bio research facility somewhere, chewed through whatever was keeping the bugs in.'

'That's why the transports from Earth stopped,' said Kevin.

Connie laughed hollowly. 'Space programs? We have problems keeping the lights on, let alone sending anything up there.' She lifted her chin towards the ceiling. 'Anyway, millions of people died, and some didn't.'

'How did they survive?' asked Simone.

'Natural immunity? I don't know, I'm no doctor. Nobody in Akpoort has died from the plague for nearly a year now. All we have to worry about now is starving and Polly eating the last of our plastic.'

'Jesus,' said Kevin.

Connie smiled grimly. 'If he's planning on making an

appearance, he needs to hurry, 'cos we're damn close to the end of days.'

'What's Ray's story?' asked Simone.

'Ray? He's trying to survive, like the rest of us. Only difference is, he's doing it off the backs of others.'

'You don't sound like a fan,' said Kevin. 'Why do you work for him?'

'Survival. Like I said, that's what we're doing these days.'

Simone wasn't sure what to make of Connie. Being threatened with a gun and taken prisoner had not made a stellar first impression. However, since then the South African had been courteous and was now being cooperative.

'What are you going to do with me?' asked Connie.

'Do?' Simone hadn't thought that far ahead.

Connie lifted her arms, presenting her duct taped wrists. 'Unless you're planning on keeping me like this.'

'Kev, unload the rifle,' said Simone.

Kevin picked up the rifle and looked at it for a moment. 'How?'

'Seriously?' said Connie.

'We don't have guns on Mars,' said Simone.

Connie shook her head. 'Amazing.'

There was a click as Kevin managed to remove the box magazine. 'There,' he said.

'Still one in the chamber,' said Connie.

'Oh.' Kevin looked at the rifle in bafflement.

'Just open the bolt.'

'Like this?' Kevin lifted the bolt.

'Yes, now pull it back,' instructed Connie.

He did so, and a bullet popped out and hit the floor with a thump.

'And now it's safe,' said Connie.

'Good,' said Simone. 'Box, knife please.'

The creation compartment slid open, revealing a large kitchen knife.

'Wait a minute.' Connie shifted back on her chair and lifted her arms up in front of her chest protectively.

Simone picked up the knife and strode over to Connie. 'Wrists.'

Connie tentatively extended her arms, offering her wrists to Simone who cut the duct tape. 'Thanks.' Connie massaged her wrists.

Simone moved to cut the tape on the woman's legs.

'Wait a minute,' said Kevin. 'Are you sure we want to do that?'

Simone sliced through the duct tape. 'Where's she going to go Kev?'

'But—'

'You're not going to try anything, are you Connie?'

Connie shook her head. 'What would be the point? I actually like the sound of Mars. No guns, no Polly, no plague.' She smiled. 'No Ray.'

Kevin laughed. 'Just freezing temperatures, no oxygen and we have to dig our water out of the ground.'

Connie laughed drily. 'Believe me, that sounds like paradise to me.'

CHAPTER 18

Daniel woke slowly. He had not set an alarm, choosing instead to let his body rest as long as it needed. The past couple of days had left him feeling drained, both emotionally and physically.

He stayed under the shower until the alarm warning him he was close to exhausting his water allowance sounded. A strong, black cup of coffee completed the process of waking up. Daniel took his coffee to his chair next to the window and looked out across the ruddy martian landscape. He didn't feel like painting today. He was still having trouble processing what Lula had revealed to him the day before. Doris's ColPol accident report had been doctored. Someone was covering up the real cause of his wife's death.

Dimitri and Lula would be picking him up soon. They were going to the ColPol station to try and see Jacob. He checked the time on his cuff. He had fifteen minutes, just enough time for some breakfast.

He was finishing his last piece of toast when Doris announced their arrival.

Daniel waited for the airlock to cycle, feeling a little giddy and nervous.

'Danny! I hope you're ready for some drama in your life.' Dimitri was as loud as ever.

'Sure, Dimitri.'

'I'll be relying on you two to grab some attention,' said Lula.

'What?' asked Daniel. There he went with the clever questions again.

'So I can stick this on an access point.' Lula held up a small white box.

'I thought we were going to see Jacob,' said Daniel.

'Sure, if we can,' said Dimitri.

'We decided that we may as well take the opportunity to get a line into their internal network,' said Lula.

'Isn't that risky?' asked Daniel.

'Of course, but what is life without a little risk, eh Danny?'

'Peaceful?' offered Daniel.

Dimitri laughed.

'Don't worry Daniel. I just need you and Dimitri to keep attention on you while I fit the data-tap.'

'We'll keep the fascists busy, won't we Danny?'

'I don't know,' said Daniel.

Dimitri frowned briefly. 'Sure you do. We have to find out about Doris, no?'

Daniel looked for some resolve and found it in the kernel of anger he had uncovered yesterday. He focused on it, allowing the rage that had been directionless to find a new target in the faceless members of ColPol.

'Yes.' Daniel was surprised at the steel in his own voice.

The drive to the ColPol building seemed to take no time at

all. Daniel felt nervous energy twisting his stomach as Lula brought the rover to a halt near the main airlock.

Lula opened the drivers door. 'Ready?'

Daniel nodded.

'Let's go,' said Dimitri.

When they reached the airlock, Dimitri leaned on a large blue switch situated below a weather-worn speaker.

The calm, even voice of a Pol-AI crackled from the speaker. 'Please state your business, colonist.'

'Hey fascists, let us in.'

With an exasperated sigh, Lula pushed her husband to one side.

'We are here to see officer Reims,' said Lula.

A few moments passed before the single word response: 'Standby.'

A green light came on and the outer airlock door opened, allowing them inside. Daniel was glad he was entering the building by choice this time.

Once they were through the airlock, Dimitri stomped up to the main desk. Daniel followed and saw the officer on duty warily watching them approach. He had one hand below the desk, probably on his taser.

'Hey, we're here to see Reims,' said Dimitri.

'Officer Reims is in interrogation at the moment, Dimitri. Tell me what you want.'

Dimitri feigned a hurt expression. 'What's with the attitude Baxter? I thought we were friends?'

'Friends? That's the last thing we are Ivankov.'

Daniel interrupted, trying to defuse the situation. 'Look, we just want to see my son-in-law, Jacob Aarons.'

Officer Baxter switched his attention to Daniel. 'Aarons, huh? No-one is getting to see that traitor.'

Dimitri's nostrils flared. 'Traitor? Bullshit. You fascists are persecuting an innocent man.'

Baxters arm tensed, presumably readying his taser below the desk.

Lula put one hand on each man's shoulder. 'Calm down boys, it's time to go.'

'You're lucky I have places to be,' said Dimitri.

Baxter deliberately put his hand holding his taser on top of the desk. 'Get him out of here, Lula.'

'Come on, big guy,' said Daniel. 'Time to go.'

Lula and Daniel shepherded Dimitri into the airlock under the watchful eye of the ColPol officer. Once they had made it back into the rover, Dimitri's belligerent facade fell away and he grinned broadly.

'You're crazy,' said Daniel.

'He's Dimitri,' said Lula.

Lula pulled her laptop out from beside the seat. 'Looks like the data-tap is up. I've got an AI monitoring network traffic. It'll alert us if it finds anything matching the search parameters.'

'Which are?' asked Daniel.

'It's working on a multi-level Neimburg heuristic—'

'Dimitri speak, please,' said Dimitri.

Lula looked at them both and sighed. 'Anything about Jacob and/or Doris's "accident".'

'Good,' said Daniel. 'Although, I'm not sure I want to know.'

'Are you serious?' asked Dimitri.

'Serious or not, we're not discussing this outside the ColPol headquarters.' Lula stowed her laptop and started the rover.

'Can you take me home, please?' asked Daniel.

Lula nodded. 'Of course. The monitoring AI will send me and your hab-AI an alert if it finds anything.'

CHAPTER 19

Kevin passed the wine bottle to Connie.

'Thanks.' Connie took a swig of the Martian chardonnay. 'Not bad. I think I might like Mars.'

The three of them were sitting on blue and white striped deck chairs in between the two long rows of giant grey cubes. Next to them was their Box, its 'door' open.

'This place' – Connie waved the bottle around her head in a circle – 'is amazing.'

'Amazing and mysterious,' said Kevin.

'You have no idea who built it?' asked Connie.

'I'm assuming Aliens,' said Kevin.

Simone nodded. 'This technology is so far beyond ours.'

'So, it's little green men then.' Connie took another swig of wine.

'We don't know what colour they are,' said Simone.

'Or what size,' said Kevin.

'Oh, I think we can speculate that they are roughly the same size as us,' said Simone. 'The Box design seems to bear that out.'

Kevin nodded. 'Ah, right. Hadn't thought of that.'

'Little green men or big purple blobs. I suppose it

doesn't matter unless they want their box back.' Connie passed the bottle to Simone.

'No thanks.' Simone held up her glass of juice.

Connie shrugged and redirected the bottle to Kevin. 'Do you guys have a plan?'

Kevin accepted the bottle from Connie. 'Plan? We've just been going with the flow.'

'Ignore him. We had planned to get some spare parts from Earth and then head back to the colony,' said Simone.

'And look how that turned out,' said Kevin.

'Sorry. But you wouldn't have found much anyway,' said Connie.

Simone smiled ruefully. 'I guess not. We didn't factor a plastic eating superbug into our plans.'

'Speaking of which. We should spray ourselves with some anti-bac,' said Connie.

'Right. Back in a minute.' Simone stood, stretched, and stepped back into the Box.

Kevin and Connie had passed the bottle back and forth a couple of times before Simone re-emerged carrying a white can labelled 'Broad-spectrum antibacterial spray' in bright blue letters in one hand, and another bottle of wine in the other.

'This is for you.' Simone threw the can at Kevin who watched as it bounced off his arm and rolled away.

Connie finished draining the first bottle of wine, belched and said, 'Skilful.'

Kevin hauled himself to his feet and recovered the can. Then, he vigorously shook it and motioned for Connie to stand. She obliged and allowed Kevin to spray her from head to toe with the antibacterial.

'I asked the Box to disinfect everything inside as well,' said Simone. 'Don't want to take the bug back to Mars.'

'Hell, no.' Kevin finished spraying Connie, tossed her the can and raised his arms, letting her return the favour. 'That'd be fatal. There's a lot of plastic in vital colony systems.'

Simone sat down and twisted the top off the bottle she was carrying. 'Seconds, anyone?'

'Thanks, Sim.' Kevin accepted the bottle.

'We'll head back to Mars tomorrow, after a good night's sleep,' said Simone. 'I really don't think I can face dealing with colony bureaucracy today.'

'I hear you,' said Kevin.

'Maybe you can tell me more about my future new home,' said Connie.

'What do you want to know?' asked Simone.

'Who runs things?'

'The council,' said Kevin.

'Sounds suitably bureaucratic,' said Connie with a smile.

'Believe me, they are,' said Simone. She yawned, stretching her arms wide. 'I think that's it for me. I'm off to bed.'

'G'night, Sim,' said Kevin.

'The Box has created sleeping compartments for us. Mine will be the one with the door shut.'

'Thankyou, Simone,' said Connie gravely. 'I appreciate the trust both of you are showing me.'

Simone returned the smile warmly. 'I'm a believer in the fundamental humanity in everyone.'

'And I just do what my big sister says,' said Kevin.

This drew a laugh from Connie.

'It's the natural order of things. Goodnight. I'll see you both tomorrow.' Simone turned and disappeared back inside the Box.

Connie offered the bottle to Kevin.

'I actually think I've had enough,' said Kevin.

'Me too,' said Connie. She put the bottle down next to her chair.

They sat in silence. Kevin was a little surprised at the speed with which Connie had ingratiated herself with Simone. He was all too familiar with his failings. He was all too eager to trust a pretty face. Simone had always seemed to discern the true character of the women in his life. At least two of his disastrous relationships could have been avoided if he had trusted his sister when she had told him his girlfriend was no good for him.

It was Connie who broke the silence. 'Is there really no way out of this place?'

'No. Like we said, big blue barriers.'

'Damn. I'd like to see what's outside.'

'Outside?'

'Yes. I mean, this isn't on Earth or Mars, right?'

Kevin nodded. 'The gravity's wrong.'

'There must be a whole new world out there.'

'You're assuming it's worth seeing,' said Kevin.

'What? An undiscovered world? Why would you not want to see it?'

Kevin stopped to think about that. He had made the assumption that the surface of whatever world they were on would be like home – bleak and desolate. But, what if it wasn't? What if it was as full of life as Earth?

'Well?' asked Connie.

'You're right. I should want to see it. I'd been thinking of this place as a big hab.'

'Big hab?' Connie's expression was puzzled.

'Back home. If you're not in a hab, the atmosphere is too thin to breathe and it's bastard cold.'

'Oh, I see.' Connie flashed him a smile. 'I'm imagining a jungle. Like the one's back home.'

'A jungle? Complete with, uh, tigers?'

'Don't be daft. There aren't any tigers in Africa.'

'Probably not any here either,' said Kevin.

They were both quiet for a minute before Connie asked 'Have you named it?'

'Named what?'

'This world we're on,' said Connie.

'Uh, no.'

'You've got to give it a name. Discoverer's prerogative.'

'I don't know. Kev's world?'

Connie's laugh was warm and genuine. 'I think your sister would have something to say about that.'

Kevin couldn't help grinning. 'You're probably right.' His gaze met Connie's and they shared a few seconds of companionable silence. This then stretched into a few more seconds of silence which were more loaded with tension than comfortable. Kevin looked away from her dark brown eyes. Had she felt it too?

'Time for bed,' said Connie.

Kevin felt a tingle of excitement shoot from his head to his toes. Then, he realised she was probably just talking about going to sleep. 'Umm, right.' Or was she? It was with a sense of trepidation that he followed Connie into the Box. Trepidation which morphed into a mix of disappointment and relief when she went into her sleeping compartment and closed the door without even a backward glance.

* * *

The next morning, Kevin was woken by the sound of voices next door. His head felt full of cotton wool and his mouth was as dry as the Tharsis plain. He stumbled into his colony coverall and out of his tiny sleeping compartment.

His sister and Connie were sat at the table drinking fresh coffee.

'Good morning,' said Simone.

'Ugh,' said Kevin, wittily.

Connie picked up her coffee and took a sip; her eyes crinkled with amusement over the cups rim.

Simone poured him a cup of coffee which he accepted gratefully.

'We've been talking about Kev's world,' said Simone.

Kevin almost choked on his drink.

Simone continued, pretending to be oblivious to Kevin's beverage troubles. 'I have to admit, I think the name may need revisiting.'

Connie lowered her coffee cup revealing a wide grin.

'Putting the matter of the name aside, Connie has suggested we try and see some more of Kev's world.'

'See more of?' asked Kevin.

'We can use this magnificent machine to go outside,' said Connie.

'And I think we should do it,' said Simone.

'You want to be first again?' asked Kevin.

'Of course.'

Kevin thought that Simone wouldn't listen to his quite reasonable fear of the unknown, but decided to try changing her mind anyway. 'Shouldn't we get back home? Doctor Webb and his team can take care of any exploration to be done here.'

'Doctor Webb.' His sister's voice was flat.

'Yes, he's leading the study,' said Kevin.

Simone's expression was unreadable. 'The trouble with that is that the Box only listens to me, or who I tell it to listen to.'

'You're not keen on this Webb guy then?' asked Connie.

'Not sure what gave you that impression,' said Kevin. He wondered what Webb had done to deserve his sister's enmity.

'He heads the council committee that is responsible for project funding,' said Simone.

'And that means?' asked Connie.

'He's responsible for the Program going down the tubes, ' said Kevin. He now realised why Simone hated Webb.

'The Program?' asked Connie.

'A gene-editing project. The idea is we get to go on the surface without a mask this century.'

'Not just that. But yes, largely correct,' said Simone.

'Wow.' Connie nodded at Simone. 'Amazing.'

'My sister is the family genius,' said Kevin.

'Obviously,' Connie said drily.

'My brother's work is just as important for the day to day running of the colony,' said Simone.

'And that is?' asked Connie

'Water miner,' said Kevin.

Connie raised an eyebrow. 'Mining?'

'There's not much in the way of surface water on Mars, with the exception of the poles of course, so we process water-bearing rocks,' said Kevin.

'It sounds so different,' said Connie.

Kevin refilled everyone's cup. 'How about you Connie? What did you do before?'

'Before you kidnapped me or before Polly?'

'Before everything went wrong on Earth,' said Simone.

Connie was silent for a moment before answering in a quiet voice. 'I was a ranger in the AWDF.'

'What's that?' asked Kevin.

Connie looked down at the table. Her reply was clipped and tense.'The African Wildlife Defence Force.'

Simone reached out, touching the other woman's hand. 'Did something happen?'

Connie did not pull away, instead she lifted her head and looked steadily at Simone. 'I'd rather not talk about it.'

The two women looked into each other's eyes for long enough to make Kevin feel a little uncomfortable. He coughed then changed the subject. 'We're going to do some exploring then?'

'Yes.' Simone stood up. 'Box, move outside this place.'

'That's all it takes?' asked Connie. 'What now? Do we go outside?'

Simone just smiled. 'Box, show the outside.'

The screen flicked into life. Kevin looked in fascination at his first glimpse of a truly alien world. He didn't really count Earth as alien despite having lived all his life on Mars.

The screen was filled with a vision of cascading water crashing into a large lake. The rocks surrounding the lake were slick with water and what might be small plants were growing in the cracks. A pale yellow sun sent light sparkling through water droplets, creating a rainbow that arced across the base of the falling water.

All three of them just stared at the high definition image until Kevin said, 'Wow.'

'Now can we go outside?' asked Connie.

'Just a couple more things,' said Simone. 'Box, give us a three sixty view of the outside.'

Kevin heard Connie gasp as the wall to either side of the screen quickly formed into more screen, extending it until the screen completely circled the room, showing the view all around the Box.

He echoed Connie's gasp as he saw what was dominating the view on one side. A wide expanse of water; more water than Kevin had ever seen in his life. A nearby waterfall tumbled into the lake and a carpet of lush green grass extended out to the rocky shoreline. Opposite this stunning view, some distance from them was a long, white wall which stretched kilometres in either direction.

'We must have been inside that,' said Connie pointing at the featureless white wall.

Simone nodded. 'Box, show exterior atmospheric composition.'

A small part of the giant wraparound screen switched to showing the percentage makeup of gases in the exterior atmosphere. It was breathable.

'Now, we can go outside.'

CHAPTER 20

Daniel stared at his cuff. A small icon was flashing in one corner of the display. He didn't recognise it. Which meant it was probably a notification from the AI that Lula had set up. He watched it blink, his mind caught in a loop of dread at what news it was bringing. Finally, he tapped the icon, bringing up the alert.

He felt sick as he saw the message. 'Match found: Doris. Accident.'

The more familiar message notification icon popped into existence. He brought up the message from Lula. She was on her way.

He stood up, abandoning his canvas. He had sat down this morning fully intending to progress this painting, but had so far only outlined a couple of rocks. He passed the fifteen minutes it took for Lula to reach his hab pacing back and forth with nervous energy.

He said nothing as she stepped from the airlock carrying her laptop under her arm.

Daniel found it hard to read her expression. 'Hello Daniel. We should sit down.'

'Of course, of course.' Daniel waved her towards the battered grey sofa. Was it really only a week ago that

Simone had been sitting there talking about grandchildren with him?

Lula sat down, still clutching her laptop. 'You have anything to drink?'

'Uh, coffee,' said Daniel.

'Something stronger would be more appropriate.'

'Sorry, I don't have a fridge full of alcohol.'

Lula smiled. 'Sorry, too used to living with Dimitri. Coffee it is.'

'Doris, two coffees please.' Daniel sat at the other end of the sofa. 'Lula, what is it? What have you found?'

'The accident.' Lula clutched her laptop tightly with both hands. 'It wasn't an accident.'

Daniel said nothing. He'd suspected, but having Lula confirm it made it real.

'The original record shows Doris's tank-belt showed signs of tampering.'

Daniel found his voice. 'My God.'

'I'm sorry.' Lula tentatively reached her hand out, then dropped it.

'It's not your fault.' Daniel could feel the sharp flint of his rage cutting through his partially healed scars of grief. 'But it's someone's.' The tremble of rage in his voice surprised him.

'Yes. What do you want to do?'

'Is it wrong to want revenge?' asked Daniel.

'No.'

'Do you know who...' Daniel trailed off, somehow unable to finish his question.

'I've got an AI on it,' said Lula. 'Unless the evidence has been completely destroyed, it's only a matter of time.'

Both of their cuffs played a notification alert.

'Jacob,' said Lula.

Daniel realised he hadn't given his son-in-law a thought and immediately felt guilty. 'What is it?'

'He's being transferred.'

'Transferred? Where to?'

'The can.'

'Oh no,' said Daniel.

The can was the colony's prison, and a last resort when dealing with criminal behaviour. If Jacob was being moved there, his chances of being released were not good. It was the place that those deemed unsafe to work off their debt to society were sent. It was the place to put people and forget them.

'Dimitri comes off shift soon. We can come up with a plan of action,' said Lula.

'Right,' said Daniel. 'What's going on, Lula? Everything seems to be turning upside-down recently.'

Lula shrugged. 'The council isn't what it used to be.'

Daniel shook his head. 'It's so unreal. I remember Doris complaining about some of the other council members, but this... the accident not an accident, Jacob being sent to the can.'

'Dimitri would tell you they're all fascists,' said Lula.

Daniel managed a small smile. 'Yes, he would, wouldn't he?'

'Speaking of which, I said I'd meet him at dome six when his shift is over.' Lula stood up. 'Are you with us?'

Daniel took one last look at his half-finished painting. There was more important unfinished business than a Martian landscape. 'I am, yes.'

CHAPTER 21

Kevin stood beside the waterfall with his mouth open. He was genuinely speechless. The roar of water crashing down battered his ears and he could feel fine wet droplets settling on his skin. The soft colours of a rainbow hung in the air giving the whole scene an unreal quality.

'Kev, it's wonderful,' said Simone.

He glanced at his sister. Her eyes were alive with excitement and she seemed on the verge of bursting into laughter.

He nodded in response and closed his mouth, settling it into a wide grin. There was just so much water.

'Connie, come on out and see,' called Simone.

Connie emerged from inside the box and joined them, flinching away from the spray from the waterfall.

'It's a waterfall, not the second coming,' said Connie.

Simone shook her head in wonder. 'I've never seen anything so beautiful.'

Kevin scrambled down the rocks to the lake's shore. The holding tanks at the head of the mine were big, but held nothing compared to this expanse of water.

He scooped a cold handful of water and looked at it

sparkling in the palm of his hand. 'Do you think it's safe to drink?'

'We'd better take some to test.' Simone took a bottle from the green bag she was carrying over her shoulder and passed it to Kevin. Earlier, Simone had made them wait while she instructed the Box to make her the bag of sample containers to take with them.

Kevin held the bottle under the water and watched the bubbles rise and pop on the surface before climbing back over the rocks and handing it to his sister. He then looked past Simone, Connie and the looming presence of the Box behind them at the immense white structure that they had been inside earlier.

'Do you think there's an entrance somewhere?' he asked.

'We should check the perimeter,' said Connie.

Simone put the sample bottle back in the bag. 'Or better yet, I'll get the Box to rustle up a drone.'

'Still amazing,' said Connie.

Ten minutes later, Kevin was controlling an Exo-120 model drone that was in common use on Mars. The thicker atmosphere on this world allowed the drone to generate more than enough lift to operate under the slightly higher gravity. He hadn't flown one since his days in the prospecting team of the Mars colony but he soon slipped easily into using the familiar controls.

Kevin was sitting in a chair and peering intently at the screen which had returned to its usual size. He was controlling the drone while Simone and Connie occupied the sofa, watching him.

'He's very intent,' observed Connie.

'Don't let his incompetent demeanour fool you. He can be surprisingly focused,' said Simone.

'Har bloody har,' said Kevin. He could almost feel Simone smirking behind him.

'Wait, what's that?' said Connie.

Kevin brought the drone up sharply into a hover, maintaining its position. 'What's what?'

Connie walked over, put one hand on his shoulder and pointed towards the bit of enormous white building occupying the lower left of the screen. 'That.'

'A dark patch? Let's take a closer look,' said Kevin.

He slewed the drone around so the forward mounted camera was pointing directly at the area in question and activated the zoom function. It resolved into a light grey circular patch in the side of the building, at ground level.

'Is that an entrance?' asked Connie. She took her hand from his shoulder.

'Perhaps.' Simone walked up to the screen, pointed at the possible entrance, and said 'Box, go here.'

Kevin blinked as he saw the unmistakable grey cube of the Box appear on-screen where Simone was pointing.

'How the hell does that even work?' asked Connie.

'Magic,' said Kevin. He brought the drone in for a controlled landing next to the Box before tossing the controller onto the sofa. 'Shall we?'

'I think we should give Connie her weapon back,' said Simone.

Kevin looked at his sister. She didn't look like she was joking. 'What?'

Connie looked surprised. 'What?'

'We don't know what we're dealing with here. It makes sense we should be armed,' said Simone.

Kevin had to agree with this assessment. 'But, Connie?'

'Do you want me to go outside and let you talk this over?' asked Connie.

Simone put a hand on the woman's arm. 'No, it's fine, stay.'

'Why don't I carry the gun?' asked Kevin.

Simone gently smiled at him. 'Have you ever fired one?'

'Well, no.'

'Neither have I. Connie has.'

Kevin supposed it was logical. Connie had nowhere to go on this world. He looked at her. She was sitting quietly, her hands folded on her lap and an unreadable look on her face. He supposed that she didn't look like she would go on a murderous rampage as soon as she was armed, and he actually thought that he could trust Simone's judgement over his own where Connie was concerned.

'I suppose that makes sense,' he admitted.

'That's decided then,' said Simone. 'Connie, get your rifle.'

Connie got to her feet and looked at them both. A light frown wrinkled her brow. 'You're sure?'

'We're sure,' said Simone.

Kevin nodded. He trusted his sister to make the right call.

After Connie had armed herself, they all stepped out of the Box and back into the sunlight. Immediately in front of them was the sheer white wall of the building only marred by the light grey circle they had spotted with the drone.

'It might open if someone touches it,' said Kevin.

'What makes you say that?' asked Connie.

'The Box opened when Simone touched it,' said Kevin.

Simone stepped forward and pressed her palm in the middle of the circle.

Nothing happened.

'Is something supposed to be happening?' asked Connie.

'Should have guessed it wouldn't be that easy,' said Kevin.

'Hold this.' Connie handed Kevin her gun.

He held it awkwardly by the barrel and watched her join his sister at the wall.

Connie put her hands on her hips and regarded the large circular grey patch. 'It's got to be a way in right?'

'Right,' said Simone.

Connie ran her fingers along the border where grey became the white of the rest of the wall. 'It's so smooth. I can't feel a join.'

'Just like the box. Except when I touched the Box, a door opened.'

Connie kicked the wall. The thump of her boot impacting the featureless surface was loud in the still air.

'I hate to say this, but we need some help,' said Simone.

'You mean Webb? Are you sure?' asked Kevin.

'Is this Webb that much of an arsehole?' asked Connie.

Simone sighed, 'Yes. But he's good at what he does.'

'He didn't get into the Box,' Kevin reminded her.

Simone smiled. 'We did take it before he'd had much of a chance.'

'It sounds like you've decided then.' Connie slapped Simone on the back. 'Less standing about, more taking me to Mars and showing me the sights.'

CHAPTER 22

They spent a day thrashing out a plan. There were regular food deliveries from the agri-domes to the can and Dimitri had access to the agri-dome haulers. These were operated by AI and only called for a human operator's assistance when something went wrong on their programmed routes. Lula would subtly alter the AI's programming to expect extra passengers hidden among the cargo of vegetables so they could get a free ride to the can without being spotted by the AI running the facility. Once there, they would rely on Lula to get them to Jacob and back out again before the three of them made their escape on the hauler when it made the trip to the recycling plant with a return cargo of waste from the can.

The first phase of the plan went flawlessly. Lula modified the AI and then the two men stowed away on a container that was loaded onto the hauler. The journey was noisy and uncomfortable but uneventful, and now the hauler was approaching the can.

When the hauler rolled to a stop, Daniel heard the distinctive whine of an automated loader arm moving into position above the container. This was followed by a metallic bang as the lifting gear locked into place. Then they were lifted, the container swaying from side to side on its way upwards off the hauler.

Dimitri nodded at him. 'You ready, Danny?'

'As I'll ever be.'

The container arrived at its destination, sliding into the receiving bay and locking into position. A few seconds later the door at the end was opened and a lifter-unit started to unload the cargo boxes.

They waited until the lifter was carrying the first box away before they slipped out of the cargo container and into the back dock of the can.

The service door that gave access to the maintenance crawlways was up a short ladder. Dimitri took the lead and presented his cuff to the door lock. A green LED switched on and the door unlocked with an audible click.

'Thankyou Lula,' whispered Daniel. The falsified identity programs she had loaded onto their cuffs appeared to be working. As far as the AI running the can was concerned, they were two maintenance technicians.

The door admitted them to the crawlway which took them further into the habitat. Daniel looked at his cuff which was displaying a map of the crawlways that crisscrossed the interior of the can. A softly glowing blue dot showed where Jacob was. Lula had worked through the night accessing the AI to get access to the prisoner location routines. Displaying Jacob's location was one thing, spoofing his location to the AI would be the real test of Lula's efforts.

After fifteen minutes of cramped negotiation of the crawlways Dimitri stopped and said, 'Here.'

An access hatch was set into the floor and Dimitri held his cuff next to the lock. Again, the indicator switched to green and the hatch unlocked. Dimitri opened it, swinging it down and out of the way. Below them Daniel could see a ladder leading down a wall into an empty corridor.

Dimitri slid down the ladder, and Daniel followed, closing the hatch behind him.

'Good. Now, he is in one of these cells,' said Dimitri.

Lining one side of the corridor were sealed doors, each fitted with a lock similar to that on the crawlway access hatch. At each end of the corridor were internal pressure doors. In a normal hab, these would be open unless there was a significant pressure drop in the habitat section. These, however, were closed and appeared to be locked.

Dimitri consulted his cuff, then pointed down the corridor. 'This way.'

They had reached the pressure door and Dimitri was about to unlock it when the lock indicator on the pressure door in front of them switched on.

Daniel looked at the glowing green light in panic. 'Shit.'

Dimitri put a hand on Daniel's arm. 'Don't panic. We're just two friendly fascist maintenance guys, remember?'

'We don't look like maintenance,' said Daniel. And he was right. They looked like an agri-dome worker and a retired colonist.

Dimitri lifted his arm and nodded at his cuff. 'We do to the AI, which is all that matters.'

The pressure door opened to reveal a startled looking man whose coverall sported a maintenance department patch.

'Hello, fascist,' said Dimitri cheerfully as he drove his fist into the other man's face.

The man staggered back, dropping his toolkit and lifting his hands to his injured nose.

Dimitri stepped forward, grabbed him by the shoulder and rammed him into the wall. His head bounced off the wall with a sickening thump and he slid down onto the floor, out cold.

'We have to hurry,' said Dimitri.

Daniel nodded wordlessly. He was in shock after witnessing the sudden burst of violence from his companion.

Dimitri picked up the toolkit. 'Come.'

Daniel followed Dimitri down the corridor until they came to the door indicated on their cuff displays.

'This is it. Watch my back.' Dimitri lifted his cuff next to the doors operating panel.

Daniel nervously looked up and down the corridor, all too aware of the unconscious maintenance worker around the corner. Fixed high up on the wall opposite the door was a camera. It made Daniel nervous to think of the can's AI watching them through its unblinking lens.

There was a clunk as the door lock opened. Dimitri pulled the door open, and the smell of sour sweat washed over them. Martian habs always carried a slight odour as water was rationed, but this was on another level entirely.

'Christ,' said Daniel. He covered his mouth and nose with his sleeve and followed Dimitri through the open door.

Inside, the lighting was dim. Many lights in the habitat module were off. Daniel couldn't tell if it was because they were broken or to save power. Debris littered the floor, and Daniel was dismayed to see so many discarded drink cartons and food containers. The colony could not afford to waste plastics like this.

They had not gone far inside when, off to their right, what looked like a bundle of rags stood up revealing itself to be a man. He was wild-eyed and after looking them up and down for a split second pushed past Daniel and stumbled towards the open door. Daniel watched as a red light came on above the door.

There was the crackle of a speaker coming to life and broadcasting the monotone voice of an AI. 'The inmate will move no closer to the module egress.'

The man ignored this instruction and continued to move slowly towards the bright lights of the corridor outside.

'This is a final warning. Return to the module or pacification action will be taken.'

'Shit.' Dimitri hustled past Daniel and grabbed the would-be escapee by the shoulder and roughly pulled him backwards.

The man lost his balance and flopped to the floor at Daniel's feet. 'Please.' His voice was a rough croak.

'Sorry, my friend. You have to stay here. Daniel, keep an eye on Houdini here.'

'Ok,' said Daniel. He positioned himself so he was standing between the exit and the poor unfortunate at his feet.

Dimitri stepped back into the corridor and disappeared. He was soon back, and Daniel was surprised to see him carrying the unconscious maintenance worker in a fireman's lift.

'I am improving the plan,' said Dimitri. He dumped the worker inside, then closed and locked the door.

'Improving? How?' asked Daniel.

Dimitri removed the maintenance workers cuff. 'All three of us will leave as maintenance workers.'

There was some quiet mumbling from the prisoner at their feet.

Daniel squatted down beside him. 'What was that?'

'Me? Take me,' the man mumbled.

'Sorry,' said Daniel. 'We're here for someone else.'

'Poor bastard.' Dimitri put his hand on Daniel's shoulder. 'Come on. We need to find your boy, Jacob.'

Daniel stood up, leaving the man whimpering at his feet.

'This way.' Dimitri picked his way through the rubbish, moving along the corridor and further into the hab module.

Daniel followed, warily eyeing other bundles of rags that may or may not be inmates of the prison. They soon came to a large room with several closed doors lining the walls. This was designed to be the communal area of the module. In the centre was a large table, above which was a delivery chute. From the abundance of empty packaging littering the surface and floor, Daniel judged this to be where food and drink for the residents was delivered. A large brute of a man was hunched over the table shovelling what looked like mashed potato into his mouth with his fingers. He looked up, eyes glowering at them from under his black eyebrows.

'Hi,' said Dimitri.

'Who the hell are you?' The man stood up. He towered over both Dimitri and Daniel and clearly spent his time in the can working out.

'We don't want any trouble,' said Daniel.

'You have cuffs,' said the man, taking a step towards them.

Daniel involuntarily took a step back. 'We're just looking for a friend.'

The man fixed Daniel with an icy stare. 'You've found trouble.' He deliberately pushed the sleeves of his orange prisoners coverall up, exposing two thick, muscled forearms.

'Friend, there is no need for trouble,' said Dimitri.

The inmate shifted his attention to Dimitri, taking another step closer. 'I'm no friend of yours.'

Dimitri pulled a plastic bottle from his pocket. 'I brought you a gift. So maybe we don't have to be enemies?'

'Gift?'

Dimitri put the bottle on the edge of the centre table and backed away, joining Daniel closer to the open doorway.

The man's brow furrowed as he snatched the bottle from the table. Opening it, he sniffed suspiciously at the contents. Then his face lit up with a wide, gap-toothed smile before he took a deep swig from the bottle.

He made a satisfied lip smacking noise and wiped his mouth with the back of his hand. 'Okay. We're not enemies.'

'Maybe you can help us out,' said Dimitri.

The man said nothing and took another, smaller, swig from the bottle.

'We're looking for a new prisoner,' said Daniel.

'The new guy?'

Daniel held his hand out at shoulder height. 'About so tall. Brown hair.'

'What do you want with him?'

Daniel exchanged a nervous glance with Dimitri.

'That's none of your business,' said Dimitri.

'Wrong. Anything that goes on here is my business.'

Daniel was beginning to suspect that there was more to this man than muscle.

'Where does that leave us?' asked Daniel.

'That leaves you telling me what you want with the new guy.'

Daniel looked at his companion. 'Dimitri?'

'What the hell.' Dimitri shrugged. 'We're busting him out.'

The man put the bottle of booze in the pocket of his coveralls and looked at them both appraisingly. 'You don't look insane. Although, coming in here suggests you are.'

'We're not,' said Daniel.

'If you have a way of getting someone out, then you can take me.'

'We have a way of getting someone out,' said Dimitri.

'Then we have a problem.' The man pulled a piece of sharpened metal from his pocket. He held the shiv at his side, arms loose.

'Wait a minute.' Daniel raised his hands. 'Maybe we can sort something out. We must be able to do something, right Dimitri?'

Dimitri hesitated.

'The cuff,' said Daniel.

Dimitri nodded. 'Yes. Of course.' He tossed the maintenance worker's cuff onto the tabletop. 'This should open the doors around here.'

The man scooped the cuff off the table and examined it. 'Nice. Doesn't help me get out of the can though. I'm thinking you boys have transport. Maybe even help on the outside.'

Dimitri nodded. 'We can help you. But we're not leaving without Jacob.'

The man nodded. 'If you can get me out of here, I'll make sure you get what you want.'

'Great,' said Daniel.

'Wait here.'

'Uh, okay,' said Daniel.

The prisoner walked to one of the doors and palmed the panel. The door stuttered slightly before opening fully allowing him through.

Daniel leaned in towards Dimitri and whispered, 'You think we can trust him?'

Dimitri rubbed his forehead. 'I don't know. But for the moment I guess we'll go along with it.'

CHAPTER 23

'That's it? We're there?' asked Connie.

'Should be,' said Simone. 'Box, Show us the external view please.'

The wall screen switched to a view of the inside of a rocky cave. Kevin recognised it as sector seven in the water mine where he had first discovered the Box. It looked different now; all the equipment and people were gone. He supposed once the Box had gone, there was no reason for them to stay.

Kevin passed Connie a mask and tank-belt. 'You'll need these.'

'Oh. Can you?' Connie held the belt out.

'Sure.' Kevin took the belt and fitted it around her waist. He was intensely aware of Connie's proximity and smell; a mixture of stale sweat and dust. He then explained the belt indicators as he helped her with the mask and adjusted the straps for a comfortable fit.

'Thanks,' said Connie. 'Oh.' She seemed surprised at the mask speaker transmitting her voice.

'You get used to it,' said Kevin. He handed her the therms that Simone had got the Box to make in Connie's size.

She pulled on the insulated clothing. 'This is warm. Is it really that cold out there?'

'The mine isn't that bad, but you'll need them when we get to the surface,' said Kevin.

'If you're ready?' asked Simone.

Kevin and Connie both nodded.

'Then let's see if anyone's missed us. Box, open the door.'

The circular opening appeared in front of them and Kevin led them out and into the Martian water mine. 'Home sweet home.'

'Hey, my cuff's reconnected,' said Simone.

Kevin checked his cuff. Sure enough the network icon was on; they were back online.

'Look.' Simone pointed. 'There's a camera.'

'Our glorious return won't stay a secret then,' said Kevin.

Connie was looking around the excavated chamber. 'And you work here?'

'It's not so bad. I mostly just make sure the dig-units are running okay,' said Kevin.

'Come on. Let's get out of here. If we're going to talk to Webb, let's get it over with.' Simone hurried up the steps, her feet crunching on the dry rock dust.

* * *

Their arrival on Mars had not gone unnoticed.

The program Lula had left running on the AV equipment at the dig site detected the sudden appearance of the Box, substituted a looped feed of an empty hole to the ColPol monitoring AI, and sent Lula's laptop a notification.

Two minutes and eleven seconds later, a ColPol search AI detected data-packets from two flagged cuffs and sent a high-priority alert to officers Reims and Conway. They were sitting at their desks in the ColPol building.

'Hey Andy, guess who's back,' said Reims.

'Mmmph?' Andrew Conway mumbled around his mouthful of food, then swallowed. 'Who?'

'Maddock and Aarons.'

'What? Didn't Aarons just go to the can?' asked Conway.

'Not that one. His wife,' said Reims.

'Simone Aarons? Seriously?'

'And Kevin Maddock. The colonies two most wanted. Come on, we've got to go.' Reims stood up and started putting on her tank-belt.

Conway put down his half-eaten sandwich. 'Jesus. Where are they?'

'Their cuffs are connected to the water mine network. If you'll believe that.'

'Returning to the scene of the crime.' Conway checked the charge pack on his taser.

'Pol-AI, log officers Reims and Conway en route to the water mine to apprehend Kevin Maddock and Simone Aarons.'

The AI's voice came from a speaker mounted on the ceiling – 'Dispatch of officers Reims and Conway acknowledged and logged.'

* * *

The water extraction facility was filled with the noise of an extraction hopper being filled with chunks of rock.

Kevin waited a few seconds for the sound of rock cascading over metal to die down, then called out to a familiar figure hunched over a control panel. 'Bannon.'

The surprise Bannon's face was obvious when he turned around. 'Maddock. Well, shit.'

The surprise swiftly turned into a wide grin. 'We weren't expecting to see you again.'

'You don't get rid of me that easy,' said Kevin.

'Damn, man. Your faces are all over the news feeds. You two are top of the most wanted list.'

That didn't sound good. 'We are?'

'Yeah. They're saying you stole that alien thing you found. I'm supposed to call them if I see you.'

Kevin didn't think Bannon would turn them in, but he wasn't sure. 'Will you?'

'Nah, man. I don't snitch on my friends,' said Bannon.

'Thanks, Bannon.'

'So, what happened? Last I saw of you was on the news; climbing into a hole in that thing in sector seven just before it disappeared..'

Kevin looked at Simone and Connie. His sister nodded. Connie shrugged.

'This may sound crazy, but we, uh, travelled. To another world,' said Kevin.

'You're right. It sounds crazy,' said Bannon.

'We were on Earth.'

'Earth?' Bannon looked incredulous.

'Yeah, we picked up Connie here.' Kevin indicated the South African.

Connie waved. 'Hi.'

'Damn. You're serious.'

'We ended up on what I think was a totally alien world,' said Kevin.

'No shit?'

'We came back to get the help of Webb and his scientists.'

'From the way they've been talking about you on the news, you're more likely to end up in the can,' said Bannon.

'Thanks for warning us. I think they'll change their minds when they hear what we have to say.' Kevin held out his hand and Bannon took it in a firm handshake.

'You be careful, Maddock.'

'Come on Kev, let's go and see Webb,' said Simone.

'Right. Later, Bannon, and thanks again.'

'Good luck, man.'

CHAPTER 24

The container was roomier on their way back from the can as they were sharing it with a few barrels of waste instead of a week's worth of supplies. The downside was the faint odour of sewage lingering around the sealed barrels. Daniel wondered why they hadn't thought to ask Lula to program the AI to ignore the absence of the barrels so they could leave them behind. They needed the extra space as they had two extra passengers for the return journey: Jacob and the large, muscled prisoner who they had agreed to take with them. His name was Eric. At least that was the name he had given them. Daniel didn't know why he had been sent to the can; Eric had evaded the question when they asked, and Daniel did not think pushing for an answer was a wise idea. The man seemed to emanate a smouldering glow of suppressed violence even when he was just hunkering down in the corner of the empty container.

Jacob had hardly said two words since Eric had taken them to him. The usually well spoken, intelligent man had been reduced to a sullen, brooding silence by his experiences. Daniel couldn't help but wonder what had happened to him over the past few days to affect him like this.

Dimitri was watching his cuff display. 'We're nearly there.'

'Good,' said Daniel.

They endured another five minutes of bone rattling progress until the hauler juddered to a halt at its destination. Once inside the loading bay they emerged from the container. Lula was waiting for them with her laptop clutched tightly against her chest. One by one they lowered themselves from the container and onto the floor of the loading bay.

'They're back,' said Lula.

'Who's back?' asked Dimitri.

'Kevin and Simone.'

Daniel felt relief wash over him. 'Thank God.'

'Get inside before someone sees you,' said Lula.

'Not you,' Dimitri said pointedly to Eric.

The big man half-raised his hands. He couldn't raise them any higher as the therms he had liberated from a locker in the can were a tight fit. 'Seriously? I've been in the can for five years. I could use a bad woman.' He was looking at Lula hungrily.

Dimitri glowered at the man dangerously. 'Take a pool rover and get the hell out of here.'

Eric turned his attention to Dimitri. He seemed about to say something, but stopped and smiled. 'Fine. I know when I'm not wanted.' Eric turned and walked away, heading towards the side of the dome where the rovers were parked.

Daniel watched him go with a slight sense of unease. They had just helped someone escape from the can. He had no idea why he was there. He could be a killer. He could be a serial killer.

'Danny, you coming?' Dimitri broke his train of thought.

'Sure.' Daniel turned and followed the others into the airlock.

* * *

'Simone?' asked Jacob.

A shot of Dimitri's moonshine and the news that Simone was back seemed to be bringing Jacob back from the brink of wherever he'd been mentally.

'The AI reported that they showed up on camera at the excavation site,' said Lula.

'Can I see?' asked Jacob.

Lula shook her head. 'Sorry, no. The notification packets are piggy-backing out on the video feed to the science labs, and that just shows an empty hole.'

'We should go and meet them,' said Daniel.

'Agreed. I will go,' said Dimitri.

'I'm coming too,' said Jacob.

'No, you are not,' said Dimitri.

'Yes, I am.' Jacob's voice was firm. Simone coming back seemed to have given him renewed strength.

'Jacob.' Lula held up a brand new cuff. It still had the protective film over its screen. 'You and I will stay here and work on your new identity.'

'I want to see my wife.' Jacob sounded like a petulant teenager.

'You will.' Dimitri put a consoling hand on Jacob's

161

shoulder. 'But you cannot come with me. You are a wanted man.'

Jacob's shoulders slumped.

'Go. I'll look after him,' said Lula.

'We'll bring her here, Jacob. Don't worry,' said Daniel.

The look Jacob gave him was heart wrenching. Daniel could see his son-in-law's eyes glistening with freshly forming tears.

'Jacob, I...' Daniel trailed off, not sure what to say.

Jacob sniffed, his attempt at a smile barely noticeable. 'Just go. I understand why I have to stay.'

'Good,' said Dimitri. 'Come on, Daniel. Let's go and pick up your kids.'

CHAPTER 25

Reims punched the button sending the lift rattling into motion down the mine shaft. Conway was fiddling with his taser.

'Have you not got the shop to look at that yet?' asked Reims.

'Not yet. The trigger mechanism is only a little sticky.'

'Idiot.'

'Hey, I've been busy,' protested Conway.

'Don't come running to me if some tweaker cracks your skull while you're dicking around with a sticky trigger.'

Conway looked up from fiddling with his taser. 'If I had my skull cracked, as you put it, I doubt I'll be running anywhere.'

The elevator arrived at the bottom of the shaft with a bump. Conway dropped the taser and it went skittering across the floor of the cage. Sometimes Reims wondered what she'd done to deserve being partnered with Conway. Sure, he was good with the paperwork, but he was almost a liability in the field.

Reims opened the cage. 'Just stay alert. Remember, there's two of them.'

'Sure, sure.' Conway retrieved his taser and holstered it.

Reims led the way towards the water extraction facility

which was the first stop en route to the excavation site. The sound of rock on metal echoed down the corridor as they neared the facility. During a lull in the noise, she heard voices from around the corner. She held up her hand indicating Conway should stop and then inched forwards until she could see into the chamber containing the water extraction machinery.

'Bingo,' she whispered.

She could see the colonies two most wanted in conversation with one of the water miners they had interviewed two days ago. Bannon, she thought it was. There was also a fourth person she did not recognise standing with Simone Aarons.

She ducked back behind the corner and beckoned Conway over. 'Do you recognise the one at the back?'

Conway swapped places with her and peered around the corner. 'No. Should I?'

'Run a facial recognition search on her,' said Reims.

Conway nodded and aimed the camera on his cuff at the unknown woman. He whispered a few words to initiate the search and swapped position with Reims who resumed her observation of the suspects.

'So, what's our play?' whispered Conway.

'I don't like having an unknown player here.'

'Should we back off and wait for an ID?' asked Conway.

Reims agonised over the decision. They might not get another chance if they pull another vanishing act. Although the video feed from sector seven showed no evidence of the object's return. She hesitated for a few more seconds before coming to a decision. 'We take them now.'

Conway nodded and drew his taser, making one last check on the trigger mechanism.

Reims talked into her cuff in a low voice. 'Proceeding with arrest of Kevin Maddock and Simone Aarons.'

Then, she drew her own taser and cautiously entered the water extraction facility; there were plenty of places for an assailant to hide. She could hear the shuffle of Conway's feet behind her.

Reims took a deep breath, aimed her taser in the direction of the fugitives and said, 'Halt. Colony Police. Put your hands on your head.'

She inwardly smirked at the look of panic and fear on their faces.

'Hands on heads, now.'

The first to comply was Bannon. That figured, he knew they weren't after him. Then the two fugitives followed suit. The unknown woman was the last to comply.

'That's better. Kevin Maddock. I am arresting you for unlawful appropriation of colony property. Simone Aarons. I am arresting you for unlawful appropriation of colony property and unlicensed gene-edited pregnancy.'

'What?' said Kevin.

That was amusing. The brother didn't seem to know about his sister's pregnancy. It wouldn't save him from an extra charge of accessory after the fact. Simone looked downwards, avoiding her brothers gaze.

Conway moved past Reims with two sets of restraints in his hand. Once he had secured the suspect's arms behind their backs, Reims lowered her taser and turned her attention to Bannon and the unknown. 'You two will accompany us and come in for questioning.'

'Sure thing. I don't want any trouble,' said Bannon.

The dark-skinned woman remained silent. Reims did not particularly like the look of the glower she was sending her way over the top of her mask.

'You will comply in accordance with colony mandate thirty-two.'

She had hoped that invoking mandate thirty-two would keep the woman calm and compliant; however, it hadn't even made her look away. Reims decided to keep her taser free of its holster just in case. 'Let's go, Conway.'

Conway moved the prisoners back towards the elevator out of the mine. Reims stayed back and made sure she kept Bannon and the mystery woman in view as they followed.

CHAPTER 26

Dimitri slewed the rover to a halt right next to the water mine entrance, popped the door open, and jumped out almost before it had stopped moving.

'Hurry, Danny. We have to get to them before someone shops them to those ColPol fascists.'

Daniel climbed out of the rover, joining Dimitri as they waited for the elevator. Dimitri was peering over the edge of the shaft as the clank and rattle of the approaching elevator cage became audible.

'Shit,' said Dimitri.

'What is it?' asked Daniel.

'I see them.'

'That's good isn't it?'

'Not if Reims is with them it isn't,' said Dimitri.

'Oh no. What do we do now?'

'A bloody good question, Danny.' Dimitri paced back and forth throwing the occasional glance down the shaft as he talked. 'We don't have long.'

Daniel took a look down the elevator shaft himself. He could see the elevator cage was quite full. He counted six people; two of them were in ColPol uniform. Daniel found it difficult to identify his son and daughter from this aerial view and found himself wondering how Dimitri had recognised Reims.

'How do you know it's Reims?'

'Who else could it be? We have to decide if we want to add assaulting a fascist to our rap sheet.'

'I didn't know I had a rap sheet,' said Daniel.

Dimitri chuckled behind his mask. 'I bet they've got a big fat file on you, Danny.'

Daniel knew this must be true. 'A virtual one at least.'

'We're almost out of time. I'll leave the decision to you, Danny. Do we try to free Simone and Kevin or run?'

Daniel considered running. But then what? Once ColPol got his children in a cell, the next stop would be the can, and they'd be sure to step up security after they rescued Jacob. 'We've broken prisoners out of the can. Why stop there?'

Dimitri nodded. 'I'll take Reims, you get the other one.'

Daniel felt lightheaded. It was surreal that they were planning to attack two ColPol officers; they had jumped over the line into lawlessness with style.

The two of them hid behind one of the surface water tanks that lay between the mine shaft and the ColPol rover. Then they waited as the elevator ascended the shaft. Finally, it came to a halt and one of the ColPol officers opened the gate.

The pair of would be ambushers drew back so they were not visible to the approaching officers, and Daniel tensed as the procession neared their hiding place.

'Stop here,' said a female voice. Daniel recognised it as Reims.

Dimitri cursed under his breath.

'Check that other rover out.' That was Reims again.

Daniel listened as footsteps moved away from their hiding place and towards where they'd left the rover.

Dimitri turned his head and looked Daniel in the eye. 'We go now.'

'Right.' Daniel was not surprised to find his voice came out shaky and nervous sounding.

Reims's attention was on Conway who was peering through the windshield of their rover when Dimitri barrelled into her, knocking her to the ground.

Daniel sprinted towards Conway, passing Dimitri and Reims as they struggled for control of the taser.

'Dad,' said Simone.

'Holy shit,' said Kevin.

Part of Daniel was filled with relief at hearing his children's voices again. The rest of him was concentrating on getting to Conway before he cleared his taser from its holster.

He wasn't fast enough. Conway leveled the bright yellow taser at him and depressed the trigger. Daniel was both surprised and relieved when nothing happened and he crashed into Conway, knocking him backwards and into the side of the rover. There was a sickening crack as the ColPol officer's head connected with the doorpost. Daniel leant against the rover and watched as the man slipped to the ground. He felt another surge of adrenaline as he realised he didn't know if the man was alive or dead.

The distinctive crackle of a discharging taser sounded behind him, and he turned to see Reims climbing to her feet. Dimitri was lying on the ground, groaning.

Reims was breathing hard. 'Daniel Maddock, you are under arrest for assaulting a Colony Police Officer.'

Daniel looked at the taser in her hand. Beyond Reims,

Kevin and Simone had their hands restrained behind their backs, and there were two other people Daniel did not recognise. One was wearing a worn set of therms bearing the mining department patch. The other was wearing brand new therms along with what looked like a factory fresh tank-belt and mask.

'Put your hands behind your head,' instructed Reims.

Daniel complied. An empty sense of failure rose inside and he felt his throat thicken with emotion. 'I—'

'Save it, Maddock. You're going to the can for that.' Reims nodded at Conway. His scalp was bloody where he had hit his head.

Daniel looked at his feet as his eyes started to fill with moisture. He felt so hopeless. Powerless. He had wanted to keep his family safe. He had wanted revenge. On Webb. On the council. And all he'd done is fail.

He heard a grunt and looked up and saw Reims collapse at the feet of the woman in the brand new therms.

He saw her wink at a shocked looking Simone and Kevin. 'I've changed my mind. Maybe Mars isn't going to be such a great place after all.'

Kevin seemed to recover his wits first. 'Get the key to our restraints.'

The mysterious woman rifled through Reims's pockets and came back up with a small electronic key. 'This?'

'Yes.' Kevin turned around and presented his hands for release.

Both he and his sister were soon free.

Simone ran to Daniel and hugged him. 'Oh, Dad.'

Kevin helped Dimitri to his feet.

'I hate being hit by those things,' said Dimitri.

'Christ, Kevin,' said the water miner.

'Bannon. Sorry to get you involved in all this,' said Kevin.

The well-dressed stranger had her hands on her hips. 'Would someone like to tell me what the hell is going on?'

'It's a bit confusing, Connie,' said Kevin. 'Apparently we're now wanted for stealing the Box.'

'And being pregnant,' said Connie, looking significantly at Simone.

Simone released Daniel from the hug. 'We can talk about that later. We need to make sure these two are alright.' She knelt by Conway and checked for a pulse. 'Thank God. He's still breathing.'

Connie was looking down at the prone figure of Reims at her feet. 'She might not be alright, but she'll live. Probably has a concussion.'

'What do we do now?' asked Daniel. He was just starting to consider the ramifications of what they had just done.

'I'm beginning to think coming back to Mars wasn't the best idea,' said Kevin.

'Back to Mars?' asked Daniel.

'We can explain later,' said Simone. 'I think you need to fill us in on what you two are doing here assaulting ColPol.'

Daniel rubbed his forehead. 'We saw you come back and came to get you before you got picked up.'

Dimitri gestured at the two officers on the floor. 'These fascists got here before us.'

'Where's Jacob?' asked Simone.

'He is with Lula, back at the agri-domes,' said Daniel.

'Thank God.'

Daniel could almost feel Simone's relief. He wanted to ask her about the baby, but not with all these people here.

'Come. We'll go to Jacob,' said Dimitri.

Simone looked at the prone ColPol officers and frowned. 'We can't just leave them here. They'll die when their tanks run dry.'

'I'll make sure they're okay,' said Bannon. 'Just give me a little tap, make it look like I put up a struggle.'

Kevin clasped Bannon's forearm and patted his shoulder. 'Sorry about this.'

Bannon chuckled. 'You'll enjoy hitting me. Admit it.'

'You got me. I might enjoy it a little bit.' Kevin released the man's arm, stepped back and swung at the side of Bannon's face. His hand connected with a loud slap. 'There. Good enough, it will leave a mark.'

'Just get out of here before they wake up,' said Bannon.

Daniel had only just opened the door of the rover when Simone said, 'No. Not the rover.'

'I'm not bloody walking,' said Dimitri.

Daniel was confused. 'What do you mean?'

'We can't leave the Box,' said Simone.

'The what?' asked Daniel. He couldn't recall exactly when things had stopped making sense.

'The Box. It's what we've been calling the artefact Kev found,' said Simone.

'Come on, we need to hurry.' Kevin started to lead them all back towards the elevator.

'Are you crazy? We'll be trapped down there,' said Dimitri.

'Trust me, Dimitri,' said Kevin.

Dimitri looked at Daniel, then Kevin, then back to Daniel. 'Do we go with your crazy son?'

Daniel decided that one more crazy thing to add to the big list of craziness he was already involved with wouldn't make much difference. He nodded to Dimitri and closed the rover door.

'You're all crazy.' Dimitri stood with Bannon for a moment, then slapped the man on the back. 'Maybe I'm crazy too, eh?' He followed the others into the elevator.

CHAPTER 27

'Box, open the door.'

A hole suddenly appeared in the side of the artefact, allowing access to the interior.

'Holy shit,' said Dimitri.

Daniel agreed with the sentiment.

'Come on,' said Simone. She stepped over the threshold and Kevin and Connie followed.

Daniel hesitated.

'Come on, Danny. No point standing around out here.' Dimitri was next to enter the artefact.

Daniel, ignoring his sense of foreboding, followed the others.

Once inside, he took stock of his surroundings. There were four doors leading out of the room, a large screen displaying an external view dominated one wall, and Simone was sitting on a battered grey sofa. He did a double take. That was his furniture. He recognised the slight tear on one of the arms.

'What the hell?'

Kevin removed his mask to reveal a wide smile. 'Oh, you're going to love this, Dad.'

Daniel looked behind him. He could still see the rocky

wall of the observation area through the hole. Kevin had taken his mask off and was breathing easily. Daniel pointed at his mask. 'How?'

Simone had also taken her mask off. 'The Box contains a breathable atmosphere. The technology also maintains pressure, despite the egress point being open.' She gestured at the opening leading outside. 'Some sort of gas exchange barrier.' She smiled. 'And no, I don't know how it works.'

'Aliens,' said Kevin.

'Right.' Simone nodded sagely. 'Box, close the door.'

Now that the opening was closed, Daniel removed his mask. Despite the obvious evidence that his mask had been safe to remove while the door was open, he felt much safer with it shut.

'It obeys voice commands?' he asked.

'Only Simone or someone she authorises,' said Kevin.

'The AI clearly has good taste,' said Simone.

'All very interesting,' said Dimitri. 'But now we are all here – now what?'

'Now, you tell me where Jacob is and we go and pick him up.'

'He is with Lula at agri-dome six,' said Dimitri.

'Do you know it?' asked Kevin.

'Yes. I think I can get the Box to take us outside one of the smaller airlocks.'

'You can?' asked Daniel. He was finding all of this hard to process.

'Better make it maintenance airlock 3C,' said Dimitri.

'Box, take us to agri-dome six, maintenance airlock 3C,' said Simone.

'Now what happens?' asked Daniel.

'We go and get Jacob.' Simone pointed at the screen which was now showing a small maintenance airlock set into the wall of an agri-dome.

'Holy shit,' said Dimitri.

Kevin was still smiling, he seemed to be enjoying himself. 'Yeah, pretty much.'

'Let's go,' said Simone. She stopped Kevin before he could don his mask. 'I think you should stay here. Just in case. Dad, Connie, you can both stay too.'

Connie nodded. 'Okay.'

'How about taking a camera with you?' asked Kevin.

'Good idea,' said Simone. 'Box, give me a body-cam, please.'

Simone attached the freshly made body-cam to her therms, and Kevin made sure he could see the picture on the screen. Then Dimitri and Simone left the Box leaving the others sharing the battered grey sofa and watching the camera feed on the screen.

Kevin leaned forward and rested his forearms on his legs. The feed was showing Simone and Dimitri's progress through the narrow maintenance passages in the agri-dome. He glanced to his left and saw that Connie and his Dad had both assumed similar positions to him.

'How far is it do you think?' he asked.

His Dad shifted back. 'Not much further.'

'I hope ColPol haven't got to them,' said Kevin.

'We could just call them,' said Daniel.

'And risk giving ourselves away? I'm pretty sure they'll be monitoring our cuffs.' Realisation dawned on Kevin. He looked accusingly at his cuff. 'Shit.'

'What?' asked Connie. She didn't look away from the screen.

'Our cuffs. That's how they found us.'

Kevin activated his cuff and called Simone. They saw her raise her arm on the screen as she checked who was calling and then the call connected.

'What is it Kev?' asked Simone.

'Simone, we need to switch our cuffs off,' said Kevin.

'What?'

'That's how they knew we were at the mine. The cuffs give us away when they log onto the colony network.'

'Shit,' said Simone, echoing his assessment of the situation.

The call ended.

Kevin turned off his cuffs power and then watched the screen as Simone did the same.

Daniel thumbed the power icon on his cuff. 'They'd better hurry.'

The screen showed Simone obligingly start to hurry, the camera view bouncing up and down in time with her footsteps. Dimitri rounded a corner and stopped. Simone almost ran into him and for a few moments all the screen showed was Dimitri's back. Then Dimitri ran forwards and knelt on the floor. Kevin couldn't make out what he was doing. A laptop lay on the floor nearby, its screen cracked and broken.

Then Simone turned, the camera unevenly panning around. Kevin heard Daniel gasp next to him.

Jacob was slumped against the side of a plastic vat, his chin resting on his chest at a strange angle. Simone rushed over and the cam showed her lifting his head. Jacob's hair was sticky with blood and his eyes stared directly into the camera, his mouth slightly open.

Kevin saw his sisters finger hunting around on Jacob's neck for a pulse. Then, the camera view was pushed into Jacob's coverall as she gathered her husband into her arms. The camera started to move with what could only be Simone's sobs.

'No,' whispered Daniel.

'Oh, Sim,' said Kevin.

Connie calmly walked to where her rifle was resting against the wall and picked it up. 'Where's the ammunition?'

Kevin pulled the magazine box from a pocket in his coveralls, looked at it a moment, then tossed it to Connie. She deftly plucked it from the air and slammed it home.

'Dad, stay here.' Kevin stood up and put on his mask. 'Box, open the door.'

Kevin and Connie moved as fast as they could, following the same path through the cramped maintenance tunnels that Dimitri and Simone had taken minutes earlier. Rounding the final corner, Kevin saw Simone holding Jacob. She was still sobbing, her breath coming in short gasps. Dimitri, however, was on his feet over the prone figure of Lula. His fists were clenched as he stared at an orange clad figure in front of him.

'You fucking animal. I will end you.' Dimitri's voice was a low growl tinged with barely contained rage.

Eric laughed unpleasantly. He held a shovel in his hands. Blood was smeared along one side of its blade. 'You wanted to keep her for yourselves. Too bad.' His eyes flicked from Dimitri to the two new arrivals. His gaze lingered on Connie. 'Oh, dessert.'

Connie levelled her rifle at the man.

His eyes widened with surprise. 'Is that what I think it is?'

'You bet. Drop the shovel,' said Connie.

'Here, catch.' Eric threw the shovel at Connie then hurled himself at Dimitri.

The shovel arced through the air and hit the rifle. The gun spun out of her hands and there was a deafening crack as the gun discharged.

The two men crashed to the ground. Dimitri's head hit the floor stunning him, and Eric put his hands around Dimitri's throat and squeezed.

Kevin aimed a kick at the man's head but missed as Eric swayed back, dodging his clumsily aimed foot. Kevin overbalanced and had to steady himself on the nearby table to stop himself falling over.

There was a second loud bang behind him and the sounds of struggle stopped. Kevin turned to see Simone holding the rifle. She was pointing it at Eric who had fallen backwards off Dimitri and was lying in a growing pool of blood, his hands clutched to his side in a futile attempt to stop the bleeding. He looked up at her, blood bubbling from his lips. 'Help...me...'

Then his head exploded as Simone pulled the trigger again.

The rifle clattered to the floor and Simone fell to her knees beside it. Connie knelt by his sister, put her arms around her and whispered something in her ear, holding the other woman as she rocked back and forth.

Kevin couldn't imagine what his sister must be going

through. Or Dimitri. He looked at his friend as he crouched over Lula. All Kevin could see of the man's wife was her legs; Dimitri was obscuring the rest of her. Her coverall had been dragged down to her knees; the grey cloth was ripped. Kevin felt physically sick.

Dimitri struggled to pull up Lula's coverall, lifting her body so he could pull it all the way back up to her shoulders. Her head flopped from side to side as he moved her, and Kevin was overcome by a sense of dread.

'Is she...' Kevin found himself unable to finish the question.

Dimitri looked up at Kevin, his eyes were bloodshot and his voice trembled. 'Fuck this place.'

Kevin felt lightheaded. Everything felt unreal.

'Kevin, we need to go,' said Connie. She had an arm around Simone's shoulders as she helped his sister to her feet.

Kevin knew she was right. Their cuffs had logged onto the network here at the agri-dome. 'Right. Yes. Dimitri?'

Dimitri gently gathered Lula in his arms, then stood up. She was limp and unmoving. 'We go,' he said.

'Jacob,' said Simone. Her voice was choked with tears.

'I've got him,' said Kevin.

'Let me help.' Connie moved to the other side of Jacob and together they lifted him, holding him upright between them.

By the time they navigated the maintenance passages and returned to the Box, Kevin's muscles were burning with fatigue. Connie had taken most of Jacob's weight, her Earth trained muscles making light work of carrying the body.

Daniel was waiting in the Box. Kevin could see his father was concerned with Simone's wellbeing as he hurried her into a chair and fetched her a drink of water.

Kevin and Connie gently set Jacob's body down on the sofa. Dimitri did the same with Lula. The pair almost looked as if they were taking an afternoon nap if you ignored the angle at which Jacob's head was resting.

'Simone. We have to go,' said Kevin.

His sister looked up at him. Her eyes were hollow. 'Go?'

Kevin could feel his sisters hurt. 'Somewhere that's not here.'

Connie went to Simone, putting her arm around her shoulders. 'He's right. We should go to Kev's world.'

If Dimitri or Daniel found anything strange with a place being named after Kevin, they didn't show it. Kevin wasn't even sure Dimitri was aware of the people around him. His friend was sitting on the sofa stroking Lula's hand and murmuring to himself. Or maybe to her. It was hard to tell.

'Not Earth?' asked Kevin.

Connie snorted. 'A place ravaged by polly and the plague?'

'Yes. You're right.' Simone wiped her eyes with the back of her hand. 'Box, take us to Kev's world.'

CHAPTER 28

Kevin could hear the roar of the waterfall in the distance. Hazy sunshine cast a matching pair of shadows from the two white wooden crosses hammered into the ground. They marked the fresh dug earth of the two graves of Jacob and Lula. Back on Mars the pair would have been destined for the recycling facility. But they weren't on Mars, and Connie had insisted this was how things should be done. His father, Daniel, had haltingly said a few words of farewell to the departed before joining Kevin a few paces back from the graves.

Simone was staring at Jacob's marker; her cheeks were damp with tears. Connie was next to Simone, holding her hand.

Dimitri stood alone and in silence.

Kevin shook his head slowly. 'Christ, Dad. Where do we go from here?'

'There's something I need to tell you,' whispered Daniel.

Kevin looked at his father questioningly.

'It's not good I'm afraid. It's about your mother's accident.'

'What?'

Daniel looked at Simone hesitantly then backed away further from the burial site. He beckoned Kevin to come closer.

'What is it, Dad?'

'Your mother's accident. It wasn't an accident.'

Kevin took a sharp intake of breath. 'What?' He thought the question bore repeating.

'Lula found evidence. The ColPol report had been tampered with.'

'Christ. Do you know who did it?'

'Lula set an AI on finding out who before she—' Daniel looked over at the graves. 'It sent me the results back on Mars. It was Webb.'

'Webb? Does Sim know?'

'We can't tell your sister.'

'What?'

'She has enough to deal with in her condition,' said Daniel.

Kevin leant in closer. 'Her condition? What do you mean?'

'Ah. Well, she's pregnant.'

'That's why the ColPol officer was going on about an unlicensed pregnancy. Jesus Christ.'

'Jacob told me they gene-edited the baby.'

'What does that mean?' asked Kevin.

'It's the Program. Simone and Jacob decided to ignore the council and perform a human trial on their own child.'

Kevin looked at his sister again, trying to imagine the new life growing inside her. He felt he should say something. 'Wow,' was all he could manage.

'She doesn't know that I know. So you shouldn't, you know, tell her you know that I know.'

'Wait. What?'

His father sighed. 'Just keep it to yourself for now, Kevin.'

'Christ. I'm going for a walk.'

His father nodded. 'Don't go too far.'

Ten minutes later Kevin was at lakeside. He had spent a couple of minutes hunting around the shore looking for flat stones. Now he had a fistful, he was sending them in a low arc across the lake, trying to send them skimming. Mostly they were sinking without a trace. It was harder than it looked in the movies but he was slowly getting the hang of it.

Kevin was worried. Worried about his sister. Worried about his father. Worried about the whole messed up situation in general. Still, he could worry about all that later. Now it was time for the wake. They had fabricated a picnic table, chairs and enough martian wine to stay drunk for a week.

He sighed and threw the last stone which skipped twice and then sank beneath the water's surface leaving nothing but a few ripples to mark its passing.

Daniel was angry. Angry that he and his children were wanted by Colpol. Angry with whoever had killed his wife. But most of all, he was angry with himself for helping Eric escape to kill Jacob and Lula. He morosely sipped his glass of martian chardonnay and looked around at his companions.

Dimitri was sitting alone on the grass working his way through his second bottle. Simone and Connie were talking in hushed tones at the other end of the table, their drinks barely touched. And Kevin? Kevin was sitting next to him. He hadn't said much after returning from his walk.

Daniel emptied his glass in an attempt to empty himself of rage. So far he had only managed to blur the focus of his anger and was now feeling angry at the universe in general.

Kevin silently filled both their glasses.

Dimitri staggered over to the table. 'Lula would not want us sitting around with these long faces. We must drink and be merry!' He slammed his bottle of wine on the table, punctuating his assertion.

Daniel saw Kevin smile in response to Dimitri's now quite manic grin. Dimitri was right. Sitting around being angry wasn't helping Jacob or Lula.

Dimitri raised his bottle. 'To Jacob. I hear he was a great husband.'

Simone looked down at the table.

Dimitri paused a moment, looking around at everyone. 'And Lula. The best damn woman in the colony.'

Everyone raised their glasses and echoed the toast. 'To Jacob and Lula.'

The afternoon stretched into evening on the alien world. When the conversation turned to hobbies and Dimitri mentioned that he used to play the guitar, Simone had the Box fabricate one. After a few minutes of discordant strumming and fiddling with the tuning keys, Dimitri launched into a passable rendition of Stairway to Heaven.

Simone and Connie slipped away when the three men started singing.

CHAPTER 29

Officer Lucy Reims stretched back in her chair, put her hands behind her head, and then winced as she touched the bruise on the back of her head. She'd taken a nasty clout from one of the fugitives. The doctor had diagnosed a mild concussion and had prescribed painkillers and rest. She'd gladly accepted the painkillers but was ignoring the second part of the prescription. Conway was still laid up in hospital. His head injury was more serious, and he was being kept in for observation. She hated to admit it, but she could use his assistance with making sense of the events that unfolded after the encounter at the water mine.

Bannon's statement had not been much help. His story about the fugitives taking the elevator back down the mine-shaft was supported by network logs that recorded cuff data traffic but there had been no sign of them in the mine itself. Then the network alert had pinged again when their cuffs connected at one of the agri-domes. This time, when they investigated they found fermenting vats and a still. Her joy at finally finding the source of the cheap booze plaguing the colony was tempered by the accompanying discovery of a dead body. The victim had been identified as the prisoner who had escaped from the can at the same time as Jacob Aarons. Forensics were analysing some blood found on a shovel near the corpse which they had initially assumed was the murder weapon. This assumption had turned out to be incorrect. It was a bullet that had shattered the mans face and spread his brains on the floor.

She supposed this would not have been too remarkable in a homicide investigation on Earth but on Mars it was unheard of. There were no guns on the planet. Or at least that's what everybody had thought. They'd be keeping that particular detail out of the news feed.

She rubbed her temples. What a mess.

Her cuff pinged a notification. The chief wanted to see her. Great. Him meddling with the case was the last thing she needed. On the other hand, maybe she'd got lucky and somebody else was being assigned this shit-show. After one last scan of the documents open on her computer, she activated the screen saver and went to see what Chief Smith wanted.

The door to his office was closed, so she knocked.

Smith invited her to open the door with a terse, 'Come!'

She opened the door and was only half-surprised to see Doctor Webb sitting in a chair opposite Smith.

'Doctor Webb, this is Reims. She is the senior investigating officer on the Aaron's case.'

Webb said nothing, coolly regarding Reims.

'A pleasure,' said Reims. She thrust her hand out.

Webb ignored the invitation to shake hands. 'So you're the one running this fiasco.'

Reims withdrew her hand. 'Running this investigation. We call them investigations.'

'Sit down, Reims,' ordered Smith.

She pulled the chair out sharply, sat down and folded her arms.

'Doctor Webb is concerned that you failed to apprehend the suspects.'

'We made the arrest,' said Reims.

'Then where are they?' asked Webb.

'They had help escaping custody. It's in my report,' said Reims.

'Yes, your report.' Webb looked down at a piece of paper in front of him. Her report she filed less than an hour ago. 'Daniel Maddock and Dimitri Ivankov.'

'That's right.'

'Two men who were earlier in ColPol custody until you released them.'

'They hadn't done anything. We couldn't hold them for longer than a day,' said Reims.

Webb made a show of reading some more of the report. 'And a mysterious woman with no colony records. Unrecognised by the ColPol AIs.'

'Yes. The footage of her is linked from the digital report,' said Reims.

'It seems to me that you're letting everything slip through your fingers,' said Webb.

'It seems to me you let a large grey alien cube slip through yours,' retorted Reims.

Webb smiled thinly. 'Touché, officer.'

'I appreciate this must be frustrating for you Doctor, but Reims is one of our best officers.' Smith had finally decided to say something.

'Then I worry for the efficiency of the colony police force.' Doctor Webb got to his feet.

'But they've disappeared with no trace. What are we supposed to have done?' asked Reims.

'The council expects progress, not excuses.'

'I assure you, we shall be devoting all available resources to finding them,' said Smith.

'Let us hope that is enough. I eagerly await your next report. Good day.'

Doctor Webb left Smith's office.

'That could have gone better,' said Reims.

'Reims. Just get the job done.'

'Sure. While I'm at it, got any lepers you need healing?'

'What?'

'Never mind,' said Reims.

'I'm pulling as many as I can from regular duty to assist. You have an hour before you brief the team.'

The chief must really trust her to get the job done. Or, and she considered this more likely, she was being setup to take the fall when everything went south.

'Thanks, Chief.'

A couple of hours later after the briefing was over, Reims returned to her desk and sat glumly looking at her screen. It was looking like she would be thrown to the wolves when they failed to apprehend any of the fugitives. The briefing hadn't gone badly. Everyone had paid attention, there had even been one or two intelligent questions. However, she suspected the end result would be the same. The colonies most wanted criminals had vanished. There was no trace of them on any camera or network, and all the AI searches had come up empty. It was as if they had left the colony.

She switched the screen off. Her headache was coming

back. She decided to go home early and try to get a couple of hours sleep while everyone carried out their actions from the briefing. Maybe one of the rovers would turn up missing or something. Anything that might give a clue as to where they had gone.

There was only one person in the communal kitchen when she returned home. Josie. She worked the night shift at the data centre and was fixing herself some breakfast.

Josie smiled at Reims. 'Hi, Lucy.'

Reims crossed to the sink and poured herself a mug of water, then popped the lid off her painkillers and tipped one into the palm of her hand.

'How was work today?' asked Josie.

Reims popped the pill in her mouth, gulped it down with some water, then slammed the cup onto the counter. 'I'm going to get some sleep. If anyone wants me, tell them to go away.'

Josie stopped spreading jam on her toast. 'That good, huh?'

Reims wordlessly made her way into her bedroom, closed the door, collapsed onto the bed and let sleep take her.

CHAPTER 30

Kevin grabbed the painkillers from the creation compartment as soon as the hatch opened. He gulped two down and then continued to drain his large glass of water. It had turned out that wine created by the Box dished out a hangover every bit as wretched as one delivered by traditionally fermented beverages.

There was a groan from the sofa. 'Do you have some more of those?' asked a recumbent Dimitri.

Kevin tossed the packet to Dimitri and requested another two glasses of water from the Box.

His dad was still asleep in Kevin's compartment. Things were getting a little crowded in the Box; his dad was asleep in the bed and Kevin had taken the floor. In retrospect, he could have got the Box to make him a camp bed or something, but he'd been in no state to do anything quite so sensible.

'Thank you, Kevin.' Dimitri had his hand on his brow.

'We gave them a good send off,' said Kevin.

Dimitri did not respond.

Kevin inwardly cursed. He had just reminded Dimitri his wife was dead. Dumb. 'Sorry.'

'No. Don't be sorry. It was not your fault.'

The door to Simone's compartment opened and Connie walked out. She was wearing pink flannel pyjamas decorated with cartoon Disney princesses. 'Is there any coffee in this damn thing?'

'Uh. Box make us some coffee,' said Kevin.

Connie looked down at her pyjamas and gave a one word explanation 'Simone.'

Kevin started to laugh. The Box only made things that Simone knew about. His sister's taste in nightwear had not improved since they were kids.

Simone's head poked out from around the door. 'What's so funny?'

This only made it harder for Kevin to stop. He managed to gasp out, 'Disney,' before being totally consumed by the questionable humour of the situation.

Simone smiled and shook her head. 'I'll have a coffee please.'

'It's not that damned funny,' muttered Connie as she poured the requested beverage.

By the time Kevin had recovered his composure, Connie and Simone were with him at the table eating a breakfast of jam on toast.

'Is there no bacon on board this thing?' asked Connie.

'Bacon? No,' said Simone.

'How about eggs?'

'Not while the Box can only make things Simone has experience of,' said Kevin.

'Seriously? You've never eaten bacon and eggs?' Connie looked distraught.

Simone put her hand on Connie's. 'Connie, dear. We have a vegetarian diet on Mars. Do you know how much water it takes to raise just one pig?'

'That's it. There's no way I can live on Mars without bacon.'

Kevin scratched his head. 'How about we organise a gourmet field trip to Earth? Simone can eat all these foods you're talking about.'

Dimitri hauled himself upright on the sofa. 'She can try some vodka. There's a plan I can get behind.'

'Maybe not vodka,' said Kevin.

'A trip to Earth is maybe not so crazy,' said Simone.

This surprised Kevin. Their last trip there had not ended well. 'It's not?'

'There's more people there, like Connie, who would jump at the chance to get off-world.'

'It's true,' said Connie. 'You don't know what it's like there. Give people the chance to come here and live and th —'

'What do you mean come here?' interrupted Kevin.

'Why not?' asked Connie. 'Kev's world is a paradise compared to Earth or Mars.'

'Mainly because there are no people here.' Dimitri stopped, then looked at Kevin. 'Wait a minute. Kev's world?'

'Yes. It's the name we gave it on our first visit,' said Simone.

Dimitri managed a small smile. 'Of course. What else would you call it?'

'I'm serious,' said Simone. 'Connie and I talked it over last night.'

That figures, thought Kevin. While he'd been singing bawdy Martian settler songs with Dad and Dimitri, Simone had been planning for the future.

'So, we bring people here and then what?' asked Dimitri.

'And then we start a new colony,' said Simone.

'A new colony? Are you nuts?' asked Kevin.

Simone got to her feet and started pacing back and forth as she talked, the words coming out in a tumble. 'Why not? It's a hell of a lot more hospitable than Mars. No terraforming required; the atmosphere is breathable, and I'm willing to bet we can get terrestrial crops to grow here. Getting a manufacturing base setup would take a little longer, but we have the Box's fabrication capabilities to tide us over with small scale production.'

'You've obviously been thinking about this,' said Kevin.

'Like I said, Connie and I spent time last night going over it all.'

'Right.'

'First thing we need is some sort of shelter. What sort of weather does this place have? Can we expect storms? Heavy rain? Snow even?' Simone stopped pacing and looked at Kevin. 'There's so much to do.'

Maybe Simone needed this to help cope with Jacob's death. Building some shelter certainly wouldn't hurt, and would help keep her occupied.

'Alright,' said Kevin. 'But don't you go doing any manual labour.'

'What?'

'Your condition.' Kevin looked away, suddenly feeling awkward.

'My condition?' Simone hesitated. 'Oh. You know.'

'That ColPol officer wanted to arrest you for it. Plus, Dad told me,' said Kevin.

Dimitri coughed. 'I'm going to get some air.'

'I'll come too,' said Connie.

The pair rapidly made an exit leaving the siblings alone.

'Dad? But how did he—' Simone made a small moaning noise. 'Jacob.'

Kevin got out of his chair and hugged his sister as she started to cry. He felt her body jerk with sobs before she pulled back slightly, wiping her eyes and sniffing back the tears.

'He's gone, Kev. How can he be gone?'

Kevin didn't know how to answer.

'I have to be strong. For our little boy.'

'It's a boy?' asked Kevin.

'It was Jacob's choice.'

'I'm going to be an uncle,' said Kevin. He'd always known he would be. There was no way Dad would have rested until Jacob and Simone continued the family name. But not like this. On an alien world after Jacob had been murdered.

Simone gently pushed away from Kevin. 'You'll make a damn fine uncle, Kev.'

'Thanks for the vote of confidence.'

Simone wiped her eyes with the back of her hand and mustered a faint smile. 'No problem little brother.'

'You really want to do this. Founding a colony,' said Kevin.

'Yes. I don't want Webb getting his hands on my son.'

'Because he's gene-edited,' said Kevin.

Simone nodded. 'Yes. With Jacob out of the picture he'd probably spin it as being in the best interests of the baby to take him into protective council custody.'

Webb. Kevin wanted to tell Simone what Dad had told

him about their mothers accident not being an accident.
'Simone. There's something I have to tell you.'

Simone frowned slightly. 'You sound serious.'

'You can't let Dad know you heard it from me,' said
Kevin.

'Kev. What is it?'

Kevin wiped his hands on his trousers. They'd become
unaccountably sweaty. 'Lula found something strange in
the ColPol report about Mum's accident.'

'Go on.'

'Sim. It wasn't an accident. The record had been
modified. By Webb.'

'Webb?'

Kevin nodded.

'I mean, he's blocked the Program since Mum died;
but...' Simone frowned.

'Lula set up an AI to find out who had modified the
accident record. It found someone.'

'Webb.' Simone's voice was full of fresh loathing.

'I couldn't keep this from you, but please, don't tell
Dad.'

'Why doesn't he want to tell me?'

'Uh. Because of. You know.' Kevin looked down at her
belly.

'He's protecting me.' Simone let out a long sigh.

'Yes. Well. You know.' Kevin shrugged awkwardly.

'Don't worry. I won't tell him.'

'Thanks,' said Kevin.

'For now.'

CHAPTER 31

Reims knew that the investigation was heading for failure. The last thing that could be called progress was the discovery that some of the blood at the scene of the homicide was from Jacob Aarons and Lula Ivankov. There was, however, no sign of either of them, and the murder weapon had still not been found.

There was a gun on Mars and ColPol did not have a handle on where it was. This concerned Reims more than the missing fugitives. She'd turned up nothing to suggest that the Aarons and Maddock were the desperate terrorists they were being portrayed to be by Webb and the council. Admittedly, the Ivankovs had a murkier past; Reims had uncovered an illegal booze supply network that had been run by the married couple but nothing about them suggested to her that they were guilty of the heinous crimes against Mars they now stood accused of. In the weeks since the incident, the charges against the missing families had become more and more serious and, in Reims' opinion, mostly fabricated.

'Penny for them?' asked Conway.

Reims looked up from her coffee cup. 'Just wondering

how we ended up running this shit-show of an investigation.'

'Just lucky, I guess,' said Conway.

'Sort of luck we could do without. The chief's been shielding us form the worst, but Webb's an impatient man.'

'I still don't see what he expects us to do.'

'Perform bloody miracles as far as I can tell,' said Reims. 'We got anything new from the deep AI analysis we ran on the water mine data logs?'

'You mean the analysis we've already run six times?'

'That's the one.'

'Nope. There's no trace of any footage that was replaced with that looped recording.'

Reims was hoping they'd find some evidence that the artefact was the means of travel being used by the fugitives. It was the only theory that made any sort of sense. It was like Holmes, that detective in her favourite books said, "when you have eliminated the impossible, whatever remains, however improbable, must be the truth."

Conway spun his chair away from his screen and stood up. 'Want to go get some coffee?'

Reims spotted a flashing notification icon on Conway's screen. He hadn't activated the screen lock. Sloppy, as usual. 'Check your notification first.'

Conway leant over his keyboard and accessed his notifications. 'That's funny.'

'What? Another one of those pranking vids?'

'No. One of our friends and family AI searches has found an anomaly.'

Reims joined Conway at his screen. The report was

showing inconsistencies in an old accident report relating to the Maddock family. 'Odd. Run a more detailed analysis.'

'On it.' Conway returned to his chair and started to work.

Reims left him to it and went to get the drinks. By the time she had returned with two steaming cups of coffee, Conway was looking at the analysis results with a perplexed look on his face.

Reims put his coffee on her desk. 'Anything interesting?'

'Interesting. You could say that.'

Reims pulled her chair over to his desk and sat down next to him. 'What is it?'

'The accident report is for Mrs Maddock's mask accident six years ago.'

'She was a councillor right? I think I remember that on the news.'

'That's right. Well, the report's been altered after being filed.'

'Spellcheck probably,' said Reims. 'You know accident investigators can't spell for shit.'

'It's more pervasive. Whole sections redacted and the rest with major alterations.'

'Crap. Who filed it?'

'That's where it gets weirder,' said Conway.

'Who was it?'

'Reynolds.'

Reynolds had been forced to retire around five years ago after some sort of mental breakdown. Reims slumped back into her chair. 'Well, shit.'

'What is this?' asked Conway.

'A world of shit, that's what,' said Reims. 'Has our search been logged?'

'Logged and the results filed and flagged,' said Conway.

'Shit.' Reims felt the word really applied to this situation.

'What's the problem?' asked Conway.

Sometimes Reims wished she was as clueless as he was.

'We've just uncovered a cover up,' whispered Reims.

Conway glanced around the office at their fellow ColPol officers. Nobody seemed to be paying them any attention. He also dropped his voice to a whisper. 'Shit.'

Reims kept her voice low. 'Now you've got it.'

'But who?' asked Conway.

Reims assumed this was rhetorical. 'Does it matter?'

Conway rubbed his face with his hands. 'We could just ignore it.'

'We could.' Reims realised she couldn't. 'Is that what you want to do?'

'I don't know.'

'Let me know when you make your mind up.'

Conway stared at his screen for a few moments before responding. 'We can't ignore it, can we?'

'That's decided then.' Reims rolled her chair back to her desk. Having made this decision, she felt a tingle of nervous excitement. They would have to keep this investigation off the system and work on it quietly under the cover of the artefact case. The artefact case. She groaned out loud.

Conway looked over with a worried frown on his face. 'What? What is it?'

'We've got a meeting with Smith this afternoon. He wants a progress report.'

'That won't take long,' said Conway glumly.

'One advantage of having achieved sweet F.A. I suppose.'

The progress report had gone as well as Reims had expected. Badly. The chief was obviously still getting leaned on, and all the shit was rolling downhill. After the pair of them had been lambasted and generally made to feel incompetent by Smith, she headed home in a foul mood. Conway would presumably continue worrying about what they had found once he got back to his wife and kids. Reims considered family an impediment to doing good police work.

Back at the hab, she was greeted by the familiar smell of people and food. Josie and David were sitting at the kitchen table with a plateful of beans each.

'Hi there Lucy,' said Josie in between mouthfuls of food.

David looked at his plate, avoiding looking at Reims. He had been on the receiving end of her temper after last weeks progress report and hadn't said a word to her since. Reims supposed she would have to apologise at some point. Not now though.

'Any of that left?' asked Reims.

'Sure, help yourself.' Josie nodded to a blue ceramic pot on the side.

Reims ladled a helping onto a plate and sat down at the table with the others.

David, having finished his beans, got up and dumped the plate into the dishwasher. 'I have to get to work.'

'See you later, Dave,' said Josie.

Reims found it easier to just nod at him as he left the room and headed for the airlock.

'You've not been home much lately.' Josie's statement carried an implied question.

'Been busy.'

'We've been worried about you, Lucy.' Josie put her hand on Reims's arm. She resisted the temptation to shrug it away.

'Don't be.'

'We...I care about you. You know that?'

Reims looked up into Josie's blue eyes. They almost seemed to glow under the hab-lighting. She felt a slight thrill at the continued contact of the woman's hand on her arm. Josie occasionally shared her bed and Reims knew that Josie wanted more from her. She had been deliberately keeping the relationship on a superficial level emotionally but Reims decided that now was not the time to keep her at arm's length.

'You, uh, free later tonight?' asked Reims.

Josie smiled and squeezed her arm. 'I'll come see you after my shift.'

'I'll be sure to set my alarm.'

Josie leant over and kissed Reims on the cheek. 'I'd better bounce. I'll be seeing you later.' She winked with an exaggerated suggestiveness.

Reims watched Josie go, appreciating the way she filled her coveralls. It would do her good to have a bit of human contact. Maybe it would help her forget the shitty mess she had found herself in. Or maybe she could use her evening to look into that dodgy accident report.

After finishing her beans, she retreated to her bedroom.

After setting her alarm for fifteen minutes after Josie's shift ended, she switched on her personal screen and loaded up her AI.

Three hours later, she had her answer. Webb. Of course it was Webb. He had used privileged council AI access to modify the reports. The arrogant shit hadn't done a very good job of covering his tracks; he had even put his name in the comment section of the AI directive file he had used.

Webb's picture occupied the centre of her screen. She had pulled up his file and read all about his rise to power. It was suspiciously full of promotions after his superiors met with unfortunate accidents. She should probably run those accident reports through the same process.

That would have to wait for tomorrow. She had an appointment in the morning that she wanted to keep.

Hours later, as the sun was rising above the rocky red mountains of Mars, Reims woke up for a second time; this time unaided. She lay on her side watching the gentle rise and fall of the bedclothes covering Josie. Arm's length. Who was she kidding? Reims swung her legs out of the bed and stood up, being careful not to disturb the other occupant. She stretched, got a whiff of her armpit and pulled a face. Then, after planting a tender kiss on Josie's forehead, she left to use up some of her water allowance to wash away the smell of sweat and sex.

CHAPTER 32

Kevin pushed his hat up off his face so he could see Simone.

'Did you hear what I said?' she asked.

'Sort of.'

'What did I say?'

'In that case. No.'

Kevin was gently swinging side to side in a hammock which was strung between two steel poles by the shore of lake Crystal. They had started naming things after the first new immigrants from Earth had arrived to form a settlement which was known as 'New Hope'. He wasn't sure how many people got the reference to an ancient movie. The gentle warmth from the sun coupled with the rocking motion had aided his now habitual afternoon nap. Simone had disturbed that by coming to talk to him.

Simone tutted. 'I said, we have to go back to Mars.'

'What?' Kevin attempted to sit up in shock, but failed due to the physics involved with lying in a hammock. 'Hang on, let me get out of this.'

Extricating himself from the hammock he put his bare feet onto the short grass. Technically, it wasn't grass; it was native to Kev's world and its short blades were a deep blue/green. Simone had been talking about performing a chemical analysis to see if it would serve as grazing for terrestrial animals. That plan seemed to be on the back burner.

Kevin wiped a bead of sweat from his forehead with the back of his hand. 'Now. What the hell do you want to go back to Mars for?'

'Revenge.'

'Ah.'

Simone's hands were clenched into fists. 'I tried telling myself it was for the good of the colony. Freeing the people from the oppression of the council.'

'And it isn't?'

'It is. Slightly. Mostly though, it's revenge. Webb needs to pay for what he's done.'

'You're not going to find me disagreeing with that,' said Kevin.

'You'll help then?'

'Of course,' said Kevin.

'We can't let Dad know.'

'Of course.'

Kevin looked over at the shelter they had built for their father. It was last in a row of four at the edge of the settlement close to the lake's shore. The dark-blue door was closed. He had been keeping to himself the last couple of weeks, only sojourning out of his hut to get food and ask for more painting materials.

'I'm worried about him,' said Simone.

'He's probably worried about you.' Kevin couldn't be sure about this; he hadn't had so many monosyllabic exchanges with his father since he was a teenager.

'I know.'

'Do you have a plan?' asked Kevin.

'Yes, I do,' said Simone.

* * *

'You all set?' asked Simone.

Connie nodded. She was wearing a tank-belt, mask, and therms with a maintenance patch on the arm.

Kevin finished adjusting his mask. 'Ready.'

'Are you sure Bannon will help?' asked Simone.

'As long as all we're asking is for him to pass this on to ColPol, yes.' Kevin held up a flash drive.

'I'll start bringing the box here on the hour in two hours time. That should give you enough time to get to Bannon and back again.'

'We're ready,' said Kevin.

'Good luck. Box, open the door.'

Kevin and Connie stepped out of the Box and onto the surface of Mars.

'We need to go this way.' Kevin pointed through a natural rocky arch over a path through the rocks ahead. 'We should be able to pick up the road and get to a public rover park in under an hour.'

'Why here?' Connie looked around, taking in the desolate rocky scenery. There were no habitats in sight and theirs were the only boot prints on the ground.

'Dad used to come out here to paint. He would let us run around playing Colonists and Martians while he worked.'

'Which were you?' asked Connie.

'I always got to be the evil martian,' said Kevin.

'And Sim was the heroic colonist?'

'You got it.'

'Suits her,' said Connie.

The going got easier when they reached the hard packed dirt of the road, and they soon reached the rover park. This was the first risk they had to take: using Lula's cuff to use a public rover. Kevin held the cuff up to the rovers access panel and there was an audible click as the lock opened, allowing them inside.

'That's a relief,' said Kevin.

He swung himself into the driver's seat and performed a quick check of the rover systems. 'All looks good. Batteries even have a full charge.'

Connie looked at him from the passenger seat. 'What are you waiting for? A written bloody invite?'

Kevin grinned as he flipped the switch that brought the rover's engine to life. 'Hang on, here we go.' He purposely poured on enough power to spin the wheels in the grit of the rover park before sending the vehicle speeding down the road towards their destination.

They arrived at the water mine as Kevin's colleague Laurie was loading the dig-units in her charge into the elevator. They got out of the rover and Kevin opened one of the vehicle's service hatches and poked around inside, pretending to be doing something constructive. He breathed a sigh of relief when Laurie didn't pay them any more attention than a quick glance.

He watched the dig-unit's file into the elevator and start their descent, and then closed the service hatch, the subterfuge no longer required. 'We've timed it almost perfectly. Bannon should be out in about fifteen minutes.'

'How do you wear these things for so long?' Connie was fiddling with the strap on her mask.

'I have to admit, it has been nice not having to wear one outside back home,' said Kevin.

'You just referred to Kev's world as home.'

'We really need to pick another name,' said Kevin.

Connie's laugh sounded tinny through the mask speaker. 'I like it. Besides, everybody is used to it now.'

'We could have called it something cooler.'

'Perhaps. I like Kev's world though. Reminds me of when I first met you.'

'Me or Sim?' asked Kevin.

Connie rubbed at the mask strap behind her ear. 'Both of you.'

Kevin nodded towards the elevator. 'Here they are.'

Several figures emerged from the elevator and scattered, heading for their rovers. Kevin saw that Bannon was heading in their direction. Not entirely surprising. After all, they had parked next to his vehicle.

Bannon was unlocking the rover when Kevin and Connie approached him. His eyes widened as he recognised them. 'Jesus, Kev.'

'Hi, Bannon,' said Kevin nonchalantly.

'What the hell are you doing here?'

'I missed your wit and charm.'

Bannon threw a look over his shoulder. 'Get in the damn rover.'

Once all three were inside, away from prying eyes and ears, Bannon let out a stream of creative cursing.

'Watch your mouth, there's a lady present!'

There was a chuckle from Connie in the back seat. 'Don't mind me. I've heard worse.'

'Seriously, Kev. They're watching me,' said Bannon.

'Then it will be easy to give them this.' Kevin held up the flash drive.

'What's that?'

'This is everything Lula found on my Mum's accident.'

'I don't get it.'

'It wasn't an accident,' said Kevin.

Bannon's brow furrowed as he processed this information. 'Then what? Who?'

'Sabotaged equipment. Webb.'

'Who?' asked Bannon.

'He's some big-shot scientist and councilman.'

'Shit. So what's that got to do with me?'

'I want you to give this to someone in ColPol.'

Kevin carefully watched Bannon, trying to gauge his reaction. The man remained silent as the seconds ticked by.

'Alright.' Bannon held out his hand. 'Your mum was good people, Kev.'

Kevin let out the breath he had been inadvertently holding. 'Thanks.' He placed the flash drive in Bannon's outstretched hand.

'That's it? We're done?' asked Connie.

'Yes.' Kevin put his hand on Bannon's shoulder. 'Good luck, Bannon.'

Bannon was looking at the flash drive resting on his palm. 'Yeah. Thanks. Guess I'll give this to Conway. He seemed okay.' He pocketed the drive and activated the door release. 'Now, get out of the rover before ColPol comes and arrests all our asses.'

CHAPTER 33

Reims was on her way to the ColPol building when her cuff's alert went off. She pulled over and tapped the icon to access the message. It was from the AI that had been monitoring known associates of the fugitives. Dimitri Ivankov's wife, Lula, had taken a public rover. It didn't take long before Reims had a location: the water mine. She was almost on top of it.

She spoke to her cuff. 'Call Conway.'

The call went to voice mail. 'Lula's popped up on the network. I'm going to the water mine to check it out.'

The rover's motor whined into life as she turned the vehicle in the direction of the mine and hit the accelerator. This was the first progress in the case for weeks. Damned if she was going to sit around waiting for Conway to make an appearance. She set the public rovers tracker to appear on her rover's satnav.

Reims wondered what Dimitri's wife was doing at the mine. That's where she'd last seen Dimitri, tasing him moments before she got sucker punched. She slowed as she approached the rover park, hoping the dust from the road obscured the ColPol markings on her vehicle.

She checked her taser had a full charge, slipped out of

the rover and approached the parked vehicle. It was empty. Reims quickly scanned the rover park making sure that nobody was watching her. Satisfied she was unobserved she used her ColPol privileges to activate the door release without changing the current registered user and climbed into the back seat of the rover. Then she scrunched down so she wouldn't be visible when Lula returned and settled down to wait with her taser at the ready.

Reims' cuff lit up with an incoming call.

'Shit.'

It was Conway. She quickly switched her cuff to 'do not disturb'. She could talk to him later.

The door release clicked open and Reims readied her taser. Two people entered the rover and closed the door. The one in the passenger seat was a woman. That must be Lula.

'I have fifty thousand volts pointed at the back of your head. Raise your hands and don't even think about trying anything.'

The two occupants of the rover obligingly stopped moving and raised their hands.

'Reims?' asked the man in the driver's seat.

Reims recognised that voice and felt a thrill of triumph. 'Kevin Maddock? You have got to be shitting me.'

'I shit you not. It's me,' said Kevin.

Reims savoured the words as she spoke them. 'Kevin Maddock, you are under arrest, again, for unlawful appropriation of colony property and absconding from colony police custody.'

'About that,' said Kevin.

'Shut your mouth Maddock. You'll have plenty of time to talk in the interrogation room.'

Reims shifted her attention to the passenger. 'Lula Ivankov, you are—'

'That's not Lula,' said Kevin.

'What?'

'My name is Connie,' said the passenger.

Reims couldn't place the accent. It wasn't martian. 'And are you in maintenance Connie? Or are you an imposter like Maddock here.'

'I'm not. I am an AWDF ranger from Akpoort.'

'AWDF? Akpoort?' Reims struggled with the unfamiliar terms.

'It's in South Africa.'

'Okay. Now I know you're full of shit. There's been no new immigrants for over a decade.'

Connie shrugged. 'Believe whatever you want.'

'Turn to face me,' ordered Reims.

Connie obediently turned her head.

'Damn.' It was the mystery woman from the mine. 'You again.'

Connie nodded. 'Me again.'

Kevin twisted around in his seat, hands still in the air. 'Reims. You know these charges against us are ridiculous, right?'

He was right. Reims did know it. 'Maybe. Doesn't mean you're not under arrest.'

'We have some evidence which we gave to Bannon to pass on to ColPol.'

'Evidence of what?' asked Reims.

'My mother's accident wasn't an accident. The report was changed.'

'Tell me something I don't know,' said Reims.

'Wait. You know?' Kevin started to drop his hands.

Reims pointedly looked at her taser and then Kevin. His hands went back up.

'That the report was changed? Yes.'

'You don't know who?' asked Kevin.

'Do you?' asked Reims.

'Yes,' said Kevin.

'And you have proof?'

'Bannon is passing it to someone called Conway,' said Kevin.

Reims couldn't decide if this was good or bad news.

'Keep your hands where I can see them.'

Reims raised her cuff. 'Place a call to officer Conway.'

Instead of Conway's voice, a pol-AI answered. 'Officer Conway is not available at this time. Is there anything this pol-AI can help you with?'

Reims would be damned if she'd leave a message with an AI assistant about this particular cluster-fuck. 'No.'

Reims considered her options. She knew that bringing the fugitives in would play well with the chief and Webb. However, if she did that she had a feeling that whatever evidence these two had would be buried. Better to wait to hear from Conway. If they're lying, she can bring them in then.

'You two are coming with me for now.'

'To a cell?' asked Kevin.

'If I find out you're lying to me? Yes.' Reims waved the taser at them. 'Now drive.'

'Where to?'

'Aston communal hab.' She would take them home. Her cohabitees would be all working apart from Josie. She would still be asleep and her room's soundproofing should mean that she stayed that way. By the time she woke,

Conway should have got in touch and they would be long gone.

Kevin just continued looking at her, his hands still in the air.

'You can put your hands down now,' said Reims.

'Sorry, I just didn't want to get tased.' Kevin dropped both hands onto the steering wheel and started to drive.

Back at the hab, Reims breathed a sigh of relief; no-one had decided to take a day off work. After sitting her prisoners at the kitchen table, she quickly took a peek into her room. Josie was still gently snoring, her long dark hair pooled around her head and the covers adorably tangled around her legs.

Reims gently closed the door and returned to the communal kitchen.

'Big place,' said Connie. 'The police must pay well.'

'What?' Reims was confused. This was a run of the mill singles communal hab, not some fancy private residence like police chiefs and council members got.

Kevin smirked. 'She's not from around here, remember?'

She remembered. If the woman's claim about coming from Earth was true. 'It's a communal hab. Eight of us live here.'

'Oh,' said Connie.

'What now?' asked Kevin.

Reims started to pour herself some coffee. 'Now we're going to wait for Conway to call.'

'And we all get coffee?' asked Kevin.

'Don't push your luck, Maddock.'

'It's quite crowded then.' Connie was looking around the kitchen area.

'I suppose so. Compared to Earth. We don't have all that usable outdoor space,' said Reims.

'Or Kev's world,' said Connie.

Reims saw Kevin kick Connie under the table.

'What's that?' asked Reims.

'Nothing. She's just making a joke,' said Kevin.

Reims leant against the worktop and sipped her coffee and looked at Kevin Maddock appraisingly. She knew him from his file. The underachieving younger son of councillor Doris Maddock. Doris had been behind the Program and since her death it had slowly been starved of personnel and resources. She was worried about who benefited from her death and what that meant for any potential investigation.

She shifted her attention to Connie. 'Our working theory with you is that you somehow deleted all your colony records. Erased yourself from digital existence.'

It was the only thing that had made any sense of the way she had appeared from nowhere with the Maddock siblings.

'Is it?' asked Connie.

'We may have to reassess that,' said Reims. 'If what you claim is true, how did you get here? A secret unscheduled transport?'

'Sort of,' said Connie.

'The Box,' said Kevin.

This did not make anything clearer to Reims, so she raised an eyebrow and took another sip of coffee.

'The artefact. It can move a long way very quickly,' said Kevin.

'Come again?' said Reims.

'I don't know how the damn thing works but it does.'

'So you did steal it,' said Reims.

Kevin smiled. 'Perhaps. But not from who you think.'

It was at this point that Reims' cuff pinged a notification of an incoming call. She answered.

It was Conway. 'Reims. Something has come up.'

'Let me guess. Bannon just gave you a flash drive allegedly full of evidence?'

'How the hell did you know that?' asked Conway.

'What can I say? I'm a shit hot detective,' said Reims.

'Do you know what it's about?'

'Yes, and I hope you haven't told anyone about it.'

Silence.

'Conway?'

'Chief Smith.'

'You told the chief?'

Reims could hear muffled talking, then Conway again. 'Wait a minute. I've got to go, the chief wants to see me.'

'Conway, be careful.'

'Thanks, Reims. Talk to you later.'

Conway ended the call.

'Shit,' said Reims.

'Trouble?' asked Kevin.

'Perhaps.' Reims had a slightly sick feeling in the pit of her stomach.

'Your friend, Conway. Will he be okay?' asked Connie.

'Colleague, not friend,' Reims corrected automatically.

'Whatever,' said Connie. 'Is the evidence going to be acted on?'

'If I'm being honest, probably not. Do you have another copy?'

'Not on us,' said Kevin. 'But we can get one.'

'Who do we need to see?' asked Reims.

'That would be Sim,' said Connie.

Reims was momentarily puzzled. 'Sim? Oh, Simone Aarons. Where do we find her?'

'Ah,' said Kevin.

Connie reached across the table and took the man's hand. 'Kevin, I think we should trust this woman.'

'We should?' asked Kevin.

Yes, you bloody should, thought Reims.

Kevin frowned. 'Because last time I checked, she'd arrested us and was going to throw us in the can.'

Reims couldn't help smiling a little at that. 'That was then. This is now.'

Kevin's frown deepened. 'What's so different about now?'

'Then, you were just wanted criminals. Yes, you're wanted criminals now, but Webb needs to be stopped. You seem to be loose ends he's trying to tie up. That doesn't sit well with me.'

'You really think we're a danger to the colony?' asked Kevin.

'My opinion? No. But that call is above my pay grade,' said Reims.

'I'd like to bet that taking Webb down is as well,' said Kevin.

Maddock was getting on her nerves. 'Arresting you and "taking Webb down", as you put it, are both enforcing the law. It's what I do.'

Kevin gave a derisory snort. 'The "obeying orders" defence?'

'Maddock, do me a favour and keep your opinions to

yourself.' Reims was finding it hard to suppress her natural desire to punch him on the nose. Maybe if he shut up for a minute, she would manage it.

Kevin opened his mouth to speak, but Connie moved her hand on to his arm. She looked up at Reims. 'Can we all just agree that Webb is the bigger villain here?'

Reims nodded. 'Which is why you are here and not in a ColPol cell.'

'I suppose so,' said Kevin.

Her cuff chimed a message notification. It was from Conway. He wanted to meet her at the scene of the homicide at the agri-dome. Typically, Conway had neglected to tell her why. She would have to talk to him about information sharing and teamwork.

Reims kicked the leg of the chair Maddock was sitting on. 'Time to go.'

When they arrived at the maintenance airlock at agri-dome six, there was another ColPol rover already parked up. Conway must have arrived.

The hiss of air pressure equalisation and the accompanying slight popping of their ears welcomed them to the agri-dome interior. The maintenance passages were as grotty and run-down as Reims remembered, and she wondered what had made Conway pick this as a meeting place. Had he found out something new about the homicide, or was it the lack of AI oversight in the maintenance areas that had informed the choice of rendezvous?

'Mars is a bit grubbier than I imagined,' said Connie.

'Welcome to the frontier,' said Reims. 'Maddock, lead the way. Don't forget I've got a taser at your back.'

'How could I forget?'

Reims found her sense of unease growing steadily as they made their way towards the crime scene. Conway had sent a text message instead of making a voice call. This, coupled with the run-down and isolated nature of where Conway had asked to meet was enough to set off her paranoia.

'Stop,' said Reims. She was going to listen to her paranoia and get the hell out of here.

'What now?' asked Kevin.

'Turn around, we're leaving.'

'Why?' asked Connie. 'I mean apart from this place being a bit of a dump.'

'Just move.'

As they retraced their steps, Reims decided to try calling Conway. The distinctive emotionless voice of an AI answered, 'Officer Conway is not available at this time. Is there anything this pol-AI can help you with?'

Reims terminated the call. Conway not available? This reinforced her sense of urgency; she had to get the prisoners out of here. Now.

Reims tapped Connie on the shoulder. 'Pick up the pace.'

When they got to the maintenance airlock and Kevin tried to activate it, there was a loud buzz and he was bathed in red light as the door refused to open.

'What the hell?' Kevin tried again with the same result.

Reims pushed past him, presented her cuff to the access panel and activated her priority ColPol override. A pleasant female voice informed her that 'Your ColPol override has been rescinded pending a misconduct investigation.'

'That's not good,' said Kevin.

'Maddock, shut up. I need to think.'

Her override attempt would be reported. Whoever was behind this would be waiting at the crime scene. She closed her eyes and pictured the schematic of the agridome they had used when searching for the murderer of the escaped inmate. They were closer to the loading bay than the crime scene was.

'This way,' said Reims.

She led the way down another access corridor which ended in an internal door. She opened the door onto a green vista of growing plants. The moisture laden air was heavy with the smell of tomato vines.

'Oh, wow,' said Kevin.

Kevin took a deep breath through his nose, then let it back out again with a sigh.

'Never visited before?' asked Reims.

'No. Maybe I should have joined Dimitri working in the domes.'

'It would have saved you a whole lot of trouble with the artefact,' said Reims.

'Shouldn't we be moving?' asked Connie.

'You're right.' Reims pointed to an arrow straight path running between the rows of plants. 'This way.'

They were halfway through the forest of tomato vines when two men dressed in the blue coveralls of ColPol stepped out in front of them. Reims recognised them both. Davis and Geller. They were both brandishing tasers.

Geller's smile was unnerving. 'Reims. I see you're bringing the suspects in.'

'Yes, that's what I'm doing,' said Reims.

Davis and Geller exchanged a look. Reims didn't like the look of it.

'Drop the taser, Reims,' said Geller.

Reims deliberately placed her taser on the floor then stepped over the weapon and towards the two men.

'Woah, stop right there,' said Davis.

She obligingly stopped and raised her hands. 'What's this all about?'

Reims was gratified to see the focus of both men's attention was on her.

'That's better.' Geller holstered his taser and took out a set of restraints.

Reims sighed dramatically. 'Really?'

'Really,' said Geller. 'Hands.'

Reims extended her arms. They were still out of Geller's reach. The man stepped forward at the precise moment there was a pop and crackle of a discharging taser and Davis toppled backward, limbs locked in place by the electric charge.

'Shit.' Geller went for his weapon.

Reims dropped to a crouch as the pop of a second taser shot sounded from behind her. Geller was hit and joined Davis on the floor.

She turned around and saw Connie pointing the taser at her.

'Ah.' Reims slowly raised her hands. 'What now?'

The two women locked eyes for a few moments. Then, Connie flipped the taser and held it out to Reims handle first.

'Connie!' exclaimed Kevin.

'Like I said, I think we should trust this woman,' said Connie.

Reims took the proffered weapon. 'Thanks.'

She turned back to Geller. The man had his eyes shut and was groaning in pain.

Reims tased him again. She had never liked Geller. His body spasmed and went still as he lost consciousness. Reims checked on Davis. There was a smear of blood on his scalp from where he had hit his head as he fell.

'Shit.' Reims sent a priority medical notice to the hospital, without mentioning exactly who was involved in the medical emergency. It should take them a little while to put two and two together and hopefully they would be long gone before there was any 'officer down' response.

CHAPTER 34

The knock on the door startled Daniel.

There was a muffled voice from outside. 'You awake, Danny?' It was Dimitri.

'Yes, come in.'

The door opened and Dimitri ducked inside. Daniel was still getting used to not having an airlock. He was also getting used to no home comforts. The fabricator in the Box had been fully occupied making materials to help build their new settlement. Some of the building materials had been scavenged from Earth by Simone and Connie but inevitably the construction team needed something they had forgotten or that was made of plastic.

'How're you doing Dimitri?' asked Daniel.

'Oh, you know. Some days are better than others.'

Daniel nodded. He remembered the days immediately following Doris's death. He hadn't been of much use to anyone. 'I understand.'

'Did Kev tell you anything about another scavenging trip?' asked Dimitri.

'No. Why?'

'The Box is gone. Along with Kev, Simone and Connie.' Dimitri scratched at his beard. He hadn't shaved for weeks. 'I wouldn't mind, but we need some parts for the water pump.'

'Not having to go down to the lake with a bucket would be nice,' said Daniel.

'Want to get some food? One of the new guys has a barbecue set up.'

'A what?'

'It's cooking outside. It's a thing on Earth,' said Dimitri.

'Right, I knew that.'

Outside, Daniel took in the sights and sounds of the new settlement. Someone was hammering something metal somewhere, and he could hear the excited screams of playing children. Children playing outside seemed like some sort of mad dream after living on Mars.

They followed the smell of cooking down to the lakeside. There, they could see the barbecue being manned by one of Connie's friends they had brought from Earth. There were half a dozen other new arrivals standing around talking, eating barbecued sausages brought back from Earth and drinking the martian chardonnay produced by the Box.

'Once we have our first crops here, we can make our own booze,' said Dimitri.

'Do we need to go and pick up your still?' asked Daniel.

Dimitri laughed. 'It would be nice, but probably too risky. We're all wanted on Mars remember?'

'Thanks to Webb.'

'Webb?' asked Dimitri.

'According to Lula, he was behind Doris's faked accident report too.'

Dimitri's voice trembled slightly. 'Lula?'

'Sorry.' Daniel put a hand on Dimitri's arm. 'She programmed an AI which found out.'

Dimitri took a deep shuddering breath. 'Of course.' He wiped his eyes. 'Come, let's get some food before this lot eat it all.'

After the food was finished and the wine drunk, Dimitri and Daniel were standing in the lake, with their trousers rolled up, paddling. They were facing inland, towards the settlement.

'Still no sign of the Box, Danny.' Dimitri pointed to the large square patch of dead alien grass that marked where it normally rested.

'No,' said Daniel.

As if on cue, the Box appeared. The surrounding grass rippled as displaced air rushed over it.

'I meant to say, there it is,' said Daniel.

'Very funny. Come on, let's go and see where they've been.'

They found Simone sitting on a deckchair outside the Box. She had a paperback book in her hand and was frowning in concentration.

'Where did you find that?' asked Daniel.

Simone looked up at him, a distracted look on her face. 'What?'

'The book. Where on Mars did you get it from?'

She turned the book over in her hands and looked at the cover as if seeing it for the first time.

'Not Mars. Earth. Connie picked it up for me on her last trip.'

Simone folded over the corner of the page she had been

reading and put the book on the ground beside her. Daniel read the title on the book's cover. 'Their Eyes Were Watching God'.

'Is it any good?'

'I've only just started it.'

Dimitri interrupted. 'Who cares? Where have you been? We need more building supplies.'

'Sorry. We need the Box for something else for a while.'

Dimitri's voice got louder. 'Damn it, Simone. You can't do shit like this without telling me. I'm trying to get this settlement up and running.'

'I can and I will. You're not my supervisor, Dimitri.'

'Then tell me. What's so goddamn important?'

Simone looked at Daniel then back to Dimitri. 'I can't tell you.'

'Bullshit.' Dimitri scowled.

Daniel decided it was time to step in. 'Dimitri, I'm sure Simone has a good reason for not sharing what she's up to.' He turned his attention to his daughter. 'Simone, surely you can tell us something about what you're doing?'

Simone did not say anything.

'Tell us,' said Dimitri.

'You're not going to like it, Dad.'

'Try me,' said Daniel.

'We...Kevin and I...'

Daniel nodded encouragingly.

'I took Kevin and Connie to Mars.' Simone stopped. Daniel recognised the look. It was the same expression she wore as a child when caught in one of her schemes with her little brother.

Daniel couldn't believe it. Actually, he could. 'What the hell, Simone?'

'They're taking evidence of Mum's murder to ColPol.'

'Shit,' commented Dimitri.

'Simone.' Daniel didn't know what to say. His initial reaction was one of shock and concern that his children were putting themselves in danger. This was followed by an almost guilty thrill. A feeling that justice would be done for Doris. If the right people got hold of that evidence, Webb was finished.

'Dad, I'm pregnant, not made of glass.'

'I know,' said Daniel. 'You should have told me.'

Simone got to her feet and threw her arms around him, hugging hard. 'I know.'

Dimitri coughed.

Simone released Daniel with a little laugh. 'Sorry, Dimitri. We should have told you as well. I just know how you feel about ColPol.'

'I'm glad Lula could help you.' Dimitri wiped his eyes with the back of his hand. 'Are they on Mars now?'

'Yes. I'm taking the Box to the agreed pick up point every hour until they show up.'

'And if they don't show up?' Daniel asked quietly.

'They will,' said Simone.

'You sound very sure.'

Dimitri interrupted. 'Danny, if they don't then we will go get them. Right?'

'They will,' repeated Simone.

'I just hope you're right,' said Daniel. 'We're coming with you next time.'

'Yes. We will go with you. Make sure you stay safe,' said Dimitri.

Simone nodded. 'Okay. I can cope with that. It's actually a relief you two knowing.'

'So, when do we go?' asked Daniel.

Simone checked her cuff. It still told the time without being connected to the colony network. 'In about fifteen minutes.'

'I have to go and tell the construction team they will be on a long break,' said Dimitri.

'Hurry back. I won't wait,' said Simone.

Dimitri grinned. 'We are on a schedule. I understand schedules.'

Simone gently pushed Dimitri towards the settlement. 'Just hurry up, Dimitri.'

CHAPTER 35

They used the main airlock to leave the agri-dome. Reims knew they were lucky to catch a shift change which let them mingle with the workers heading home for the day, keeping their heads down to avoid being picked up by any AI that was monitoring the cameras. The exit was bereft of any ColPol observers, and she guessed Geller and Davis were supposed to be watching this way out.

Reims hesitated in front of the rover access panel.

'What's the matter?' asked Kevin.

'I'm pretty sure my cuff's being monitored,' said Reims.

'Not even wearing mine.' Kevin held up his bare wrist for inspection.

'Connie. Use yours.' Reims put her cuff into standby mode, disconnecting it from the network.

'Won't Lula's cuff be monitored as well?' asked Kevin.

'It is. But unless anyone has changed it, the AI will only notify myself and Conway.'

'Okay.' Connie awkwardly held her wrist out towards the access panel. 'Here goes.'

Reims noticed the unfamiliar way Connie was handling

the cuff's most basic functions. Perhaps she really was from Earth.

Reims put one hand on her taser. 'Maddock, you drive.'

'Still don't trust me, huh?'

'Forgive me but I'm not in a trusting mood after recent events.'

'I hope you change your mind about us,' said Connie.

Reims smiled grimly. 'So do I. Now, let's get the hell out of here.'

Kevin did as he was told and sat in the driver's seat. Reims took her usual seat in the back. However, this time she didn't draw her taser.

Connie looked at the holstered weapon. 'Maybe starting to trust us a little?'

'Maybe.'

'Where to?' asked Kevin.

Reims responded with a question of her own. 'Can you take us to get another copy of the evidence?'

The two in the front seat exchanged a glance before Kevin said, 'Yes.'

'What are you waiting for?' asked Reims. 'Go.'

'Okay,' said Kevin.

Reims was intrigued to know where the Maddocks had been hiding.

Kevin drove them towards the outskirts of the colony and then veered off the road. They continued over some rough terrain and through a natural rock arch before finally coming to a halt in an unremarkable bit of martian wilderness.

Reims looked around for some natural shelter the fugitives may have been hiding. There was nothing. She looked questioningly at Kevin who had switched off the rover's motor, removed his seat-belt and was settling back in his chair.

'Now, we wait,' he said.

'Excuse me? We're in the middle of goddamn nowhere,' said Reims.

'We're meeting Sim here.'

'Here? Where's she staying? The nearest habs are kilometres away.'

Connie laughed. 'Oh, you'll see.'

'I hope she isn't too long, we don't have any food with us,' said Reims. 'How's the rover stocked?'

Kevin popped open the panel of the forward storage compartment and took a look. 'There's water and tanks.'

'Good.' At least they had the bare essentials.

The cab interior was silent except for the faint hum of the rovers circuits.

'So…' said Kevin.

Reims raised an eyebrow.

Kevin ploughed on. 'How's everything in ColPol? Good?'

Reims second eyebrow joined the first. 'You did not just ask me that.'

'Right. Sorry.'

Connie's chair creaked as she shifted her weight. 'What do you think happened to Bannon?'

'Nothing good,' said Kevin glumly.

'He'll be in the cells,' said Reims.

She wondered what had happened to Conway. It seemed that chief Smith had thrown his lot in with Webb and was now acting as the councillor's enforcer. Maybe she was wrong, but it seemed a good working assumption.

'Will he go to the can?' asked Kevin.

Reims considered the question. 'No. I think Conway will go along with whatever the chief says. He has a family to worry about.'

'I meant Bannon,' said Kevin.

'Oh. He'll be there already.'

'We've got to help him,' said Kevin.

'We do?' asked Reims.

'Of course we do!'

Reims shook her head. 'No chance. After the breakout the other week, security has been tightened.'

'But—'

She interrupted Maddock. 'I'm fine with waiting in silence, by the way.'

He fell into an uneasy silence and turned to look moodily at the dusty landscape.

Reims was glad Maddock had decided to shut up and went back to thinking about her predicament. She needed to get this evidence in the hands of someone who couldn't be ignored or easily disappeared. But at the moment she couldn't think of anyone who fit the bill. She rubbed at her temples.

'There,' said Connie.

Reims looked up and was astounded to see a large grey cubic structure framed by the natural rocky red archway. 'What the…'

'Sim's here.' Connie's smile was wide.

Kevin and Connie got out of the rover and, still wondering where the hell this big grey building came from, Reims followed.

'What the hell is that?' asked Reims, managing to formulate a coherent question this time.

'That,' said Connie. 'That is the Box.'

Reims remained baffled. 'Box?'

Her bafflement only increased when the circular 'door' flicked into existence and Dimitri Ivankov stepped out holding what looked like a rifle. The missing murder weapon?

She saw that the other two also looked surprised to see Ivankov. Though probably for different reasons to hers.

'Don't move, fascist,' said Dimitri.

'It's okay, Dimitri. She's helping us,' said Connie.

'Some of us,' muttered Kevin.

Dimitri snorted. 'This is the fascist that put Jacob in the can.' He jabbed the rifle towards Reims.

'I was enforcing the law,' said Reims. She would be damned if she was going to apologise for doing her job to this idiot.

'The law is wrong,' said Dimitri.

Reims shrugged. 'The law is the law. Whether you like it or not is immaterial.'

'She's helping us, Dimitri,' repeated Connie.

Dimitri didn't lower his weapon. 'So you say.'

Reims saw Daniel and Simone Maddock emerge from the structure.

'It's okay, Dimitri.' Simone put her hand on Dimitri's shoulder.

'But this is the fascist who sent Jacob to the can.'

'I said it's okay.' Simone shifted her hand to the barrel of the gun and pushed it downwards so it was pointing at the ground.

Dimitri scowled, but slung the rifle over his shoulder.

'Come inside where we can talk without these damn masks,' said Simone.

Once they were all inside the strange structure, Reims

was startled when the others took off their therms and started to take their Masks off.

'Wait a min—' She stopped. Nobody was suffocating.

'It's okay Reims. You can take the mask off,' said Simone.

She looked over her shoulder at the opening to the outside. There was no airlock. How was this possible? It was warm too. Like being in a habitat. She peeled off her therms then, more tentatively, removed her mask and took a short experimental breath. Then she inhaled deeply. 'God that smells clean. What sort of scrubbers do you use? What is this place? Does it have some sort of cloaking device or something?'

'I'll answer your questions in a bit. First, I have some of my own.' Simone turned to face her brother. 'How did it go? Has he been arrested?'

'Uh,' said Kevin.

Reims shook her head. 'No, and I suspect the flash drive has ended up with Webb.'

'Shit,' said Simone.

'That's what I said,' said Reims.

'We need another copy,' said Connie.

'To do what with?' asked Simone.

'I haven't worked that out yet,' said Reims.

The only person she knew who could possibly help was Josie. Her job at the data centre involved monitoring the news feed. Josie could setup a download link and then send it out on the news feed. The problem with that plan was what happened to Josie afterwards. Any follow up investigation would implicate her. Probably okay if the plan worked, not so okay if something went wrong.

'You can think about it while we go and get a copy,' said Simone.

'You don't have one here?' asked Reims.

'No. The original is back on Kev's world,' said Simone.

Reims looked at Kevin and Connie. 'The joke?'

'It's not a joke. It's an escape,' said Connie.

'What are you talking about?'

'We'll just have to show you.' Connie was grinning again. 'Simone?'

'Box, close the door and take us home,' said Simone.

'Home? Isn't that here on Mars?' asked Kevin.

Simone shook her head. 'Not any more. Box, open the door.'

Reims turned to look out of the circular opening. Instead of the familiar dusty red landscape of Mars, she was looking out across a carpet of lush green grass. Three giggling children ran out from behind a small grey hut. They seemed to be playing tag. Reims rubbed her eyes. They were not wearing therms or a mask.

'Welcome to Kev's world,' said Connie.

'Holy shit,' said Reims.

'The laptop is in my hut,' said Simone. 'I'll go get it. Be back in a minute.'

'I'll come with you,' said Daniel.

As they left, Dimitri called after them. 'I'll watch the fascist.'

'She's on our side,' said Connie.

Dimitri just shrugged. He was still holding the rifle.

'I think our guest wants to take a look outside,' said Kevin.

Reims realised she had been staring out of the opening

with her mouth slightly open and hurriedly shut it. 'I wouldn't mind a quick look.'

They went outside and Reims slowly turned around and marvelled at the fluffy white clouds scattered across the blue sky. Then, she dropped to her knees and ran her hands through the grass. 'It's magnificent.' She was surprised to find her voice choked with emotion.

'Wait until you see the waterfall,' said Kevin.

Reims stood up, brushing the grass from her blue coveralls. 'There's a waterfall?'

'And a lake,' added Kevin.

'Where is this? How is this possible?' asked Reims.

'The Box.' He gestured at the implacable grey cube. It's surface was smooth and featureless now that the opening had closed. 'Turns out that the artefact is an instantaneous interstellar transportation device.'

'Christ.' Reims looked up at the clouds and wondered what being in the rain was like.

'You should see it at night. Not a familiar constellation in sight,' said Connie.

Reims realised that this changed everything. If she and Josie could come here, then they could publish the evidence with no fear of repercussion. If she and Josie left the colony and came here. She rolled the idea around while she stood in silence, the wind ruffling her hair. The only dampener on her mood was Dimitri who was scowling as he watched her.

It wasn't long before Simone returned alone. 'Dad's staying here. He's feeling a bit tired. Now all we need to do is work out who to give this to.' She held up a flash drive.

Reims took a deep breath and decided to go for it. 'I know what I can do with the evidence.'

Simone looked at her questioningly.

'I think I can get it inserted into the news feed with a download link,' said Reims.

'The news feed is controlled by the council. They would never run a story on this,' said Simone.

'I know someone who works at the data centre. She can set up the hosting and insert a story in the feed.' Reims didn't want to involve Josie in this, but it looked like she had no choice. With the chief doing Webb's bidding, going through proper channels in ColPol wouldn't work. Conway had found that out. She just had to hope that Josie would help. Reims thought she would, but she'd thought that about the chief too. She smiled a little. But then, she wasn't sleeping with the chief.

'That's actually not a bad idea,' said Simone. 'Enough people should see it before it gets taken down that it can't be covered up.'

'There's one condition,' said Reims.

Simone looked wary. 'Condition?'

'I want to come and live here.'

Reims enjoyed the look of surprise on Simone's face.

'Not just me. Someone else as well.'

'Right. I mean, I guess that would be okay. As long as no one objects?' Simone looked questioningly at her companions.

'Fine with me,' said Connie.

Kevin shrugged. 'Whatever.'

Dimitri scowled and said nothing.

Simone looked to him for confirmation. 'Dimitri?'

'I suppose so. As long as she keeps her fascist views to herself.'

'I'm pretty sure Dad will be okay with it. You're now officially a citizen of Kev's world.'

Reims gave a little half smile. 'Is that it? No certificate or handshake or anything?'

Dimitri grunted. 'I'm going to see how the water pump is coming on.' He tossed the rifle to Connie and stomped off towards the settlement.

'He'll be okay,' said Kevin.

Reims wasn't so sure. Ivankov was carrying a grudge against her. She just hoped that he could let it go when she and Josie settled here for good.

'Shall we go?' asked Simone.

'Yes. It's time to teach Webb that no-one is above the law,' said Reims.

CHAPTER 36

Connie chattered about life in South Africa and how hard things had been on Earth for the whole drive from the Box to the communal hab. Reims had wanted to go alone, but the others had insisted that she take someone with her. Reims had picked Connie because, well, because she found the ex-ranger attractive. She glanced over at her passenger who was animatedly talking in her exotic South African accent, her dark eyes full of emotion. She looked wildly beautiful. Reims returned her eyes to the road. Now was not the time to be thinking like that, they were on their way to convince Josie to help them.

They reached the hab and Reims got out of the rover.

'Stay here. I'll be back with Josie soon,' said Reims.

David was just leaving as she approached the airlock.

He nodded at her. 'Reims.'

'David.' Reims returned the nod.

'Who's in the rover?'

'None of your business,' said Reims.

David shook his head. 'I don't get you, Reims.'

She didn't have time for this. Bearing in mind she would likely never see David again she decided to cut this conversation short.

'Good.'

David shook his head and walked away with his hands jammed into his therms pockets.

The familiar smell of the hab greeted her. That was something she wouldn't miss, the lingering odour of bodies and cooking. The scrubbers were supposed to deodorise the recirculated air but never seemed to quite manage it.

The common area was empty and when Reims poked her head around the door of Josie's room it was empty. The bed was unmade which meant she could not be far. Josie never left for work without making her bed.

The sound of running water came from the shower room. Smiling to herself, Reims gently pushed the door open. Steam fogged the room and a pleasant soapy fragrance replaced the stale smell of the rest of the hab.

Reims could see a shadow moving beyond the frosted glass of the shower cubicle. 'Josie?'

The water stopped and Josie's smiling face poked out from inside the shower.

'Lucy! What a pleasant surprise.' She smiled mischievously. 'Are you trying to save your water allowance again?'

Reims couldn't help laughing. 'No time for that today.'

Josie's mouth went from a grin into an exaggerated unhappy downturn. 'That makes me sad.'

Reims laugh subsided as she remembered why she was here. 'I need to talk to you Josie. It's important.'

'Sounds serious. Towel.'

Reims grabbed Josie's towel from the rack and threw it at her.

Josie's head slipped back behind the frosted glass as she

towelled her hair. 'So, what's so important you take time off from work to come ogle me in the shower?'

'I need your help,' said Reims.

'For an investigation? Sounds exciting,' said Josie.

'Sort of. Also, I have a life changing proposition for you.'

Josie stepped out from the cubicle with the towel wrapped around her and grinned wickedly. 'I thought you didn't have time for that today.'

'Josie, can we talk seriously for at least ten minutes?'

Josie sighed. 'Go make some coffee, I'll be through in a minute.'

Reims went over what she was going to say while she waited for the coffee to brew. She was going to lead with the request for help, then follow up with a declaration of her undying love and the offer to come with her to Kev's world. Kev's world? She really needed to ask if they were going to change the name.

She was just pouring the second cup when Josie, now dressed in her grey coveralls, walked in.

Josie grabbed one of the steaming mugs of coffee from the side and sat down at the table. 'Okay, mystery woman. What's so important?' She pushed an errant strand of hair from her eyes.

'God, I love you,' said Reims. So much for her plan.

Josie put on a serious face. 'That is important. How about you come and prove it?'

Reims, slightly smiling, shook her head. 'There's something else.'

Josie's mock seriousness morphed into mock horror. 'There's something more important than your infatuation with me?'

'I need you to be serious, Josie.'

'Alright. Sorry. Go ahead, what's so important?'

'I have some evidence that a senior council member had one of his political opponents killed and made it look like an accident.'

Josie looked at Reims.

'Say something, Josie.'

'Wow. But why tell me?'

'Because, chief Smith is covering up for this senior council member.'

'Holy shit.' Josie frowned. 'I still don't get why you're telling me.'

Reims took a deep breath before plunging on. 'I need your help to put it on the network with a link to the news feed.'

'Excuse me if I'm repeating myself but, holy shit.'

'Will you help me?' asked Reims.

Josie took a sip from her coffee then looked Reims in the eye, all trace of her playful mood gone. 'Lucy...I...'

'Before you answer, there's another important thing I need to ask you.'

'Another one? Jesus, Lucy. I don't know if I can handle more.'

'Hear me out.'

Josie nodded and clutched her coffee cup tightly.

'This is going to sound a bit crazy. God knows I wouldn't believe me, but you've got to know this is real.'

'Please, just tell me.'

'I want you to come away with me,' said Reims.

'Come away? Where to? What do you mean?' Josie was looking bewildered.

'You know that alien artefact that vanished?'

'The one in the news feed that was stolen?'

'Yes. That one. Turns out, it's a faster than light spaceship and it can take us to another world. I want you to go there with me.'

The moment seemed to stretch out forever before Josie said anything. 'You're shitting me.'

'No. I've been there. There's grass and clouds and open water.' Reims was animated, her voice full of emotion.

'You're serious, aren't you? This is real?'

Reims nodded and took Josie's hand. 'It's real.'

'And you've not just had a psychotic break?' asked Josie.

Reims shook her head. 'No psychotic break.'

Josie grinned. 'And you really want me to come with you?'

'Yes, I do.' Reims realised she wanted that more than anything.

'Yes.' Josie stood up and flung her arms around Reims. 'My answer is yes.'

'And you'll help with the evidence?'

'Oh, right. That. Of course. Now shut up and hug me properly.'

Reims surrendered herself to the warm comfort of Josie's arms. Her hair smelt of jasmine. 'You smell good.'

'You don't,' said Josie.

Laughing, Reims moved back a little so she could look at Josie's face. 'Come on. We need to pack some stuff and go.'

Josie slyly smiled and drew Reims back closer so she could whisper in her ear. 'What's the hurry?'

Reims pulled out of the embrace. 'You're incorrigible. There's someone waiting for us outside.'

'You have a chauffeur now?'

'Just throw some stuff in a bag and let's go.'

'I love it when you take charge.' Josie kissed Reims on the cheek. 'I'll only be a minute. I've not got much worth taking.'

Ten minutes later the two of them were dressed in their therms and carrying a backpack each. They were not particularly large bags.

Josie patted her bag. 'I just packed my favourite underwear. You?'

'Let's just get going,' said Reims.

Outside, Connie was waiting in the rover.

When Reims and Josie were stowing their bags in the back of the rover, Josie leant in close and whispered. 'Should've known you'd have a good looking chauffeur.'

'She's from Earth, and I'm driving,' said Reims.

'Serious?'

'Serious. I'm driving.'

Josie laughed. 'Not that. The Earth bit, silly.'

'Most of the people on Kev's world are from Earth.'

'It sounds very cosmopolitan.'

Once inside, Josie leaned forward from the back seat her hand extended. 'Hi. My name's Josie.'

Connie took her hand in a firm handshake. 'Connie. Nice to meet you.'

'That accent is fabulous. You're from South Africa?'

Connie released Josie's hand. 'Yes.'

Josie sat back in her seat and clipped on her harness. 'I can't wait to see this new world. Let's go and do this thing.'

Reims got to listen to Connie's description of living in

South Africa for a second time as the South African and Josie exchanged life stories on the way to their destination.

'You two had better stay here,' said Josie.

Reims passed her the flash drive. 'Good luck.'

'Lucy, please. The day I can't set up some secure network storage and insert a news feed story link to it is the day I should quit my job.'

'This is the day you're quitting your job,' Reims pointed out.

Josie chuckled. 'So it is. I'll be thirty minutes, tops.'

She leant forward and bumped masks with Reims. 'Don't run off with Connie, dear.'

Reims felt blood rush to her face. Fortunately, only the upper part of her face was visible. She coughed to cover her embarrassment. Josie gave her shoulder a squeeze, then climbed out of the rover and walked towards the airlock.

'You're lucky,' said Connie.

'Sorry?' said Reims.

'Josie.' Connie nodded towards the woman who was entering the airlock. 'You and her. Both of you are lucky.'

'Uh, yes.'

Reims didn't know what else to say. She had never been good at talking about her personal life, preferring to keep it just that, personal. Besides, having emotional attachments didn't help a career in ColPol. Although now she was in the process of flushing her ColPol career down the toilet, there was nothing stopping her.

'So…' Connie cocked her head. 'Your name is Lucy?'

Of course Josie had used her first name. She was the only person that did since her mother had passed away.

'Yes.'

'Suits you,' said Connie.

Reims said nothing. The seconds turned into minutes and then into tens of minutes.

'You don't talk much,' said Connie.

'I'm just worried about Josie.'

'She seems confident.'

Reims chuckled. 'She always does.'

'How did you two meet?' asked Connie.

'Nothing particularly interesting. We're singles hab-mates.'

'So you didn't know her before?'

'No.'

'I guess you were lucky to move in to the same hab,' said Connie.

'Not so much. An AI assigns people a singles hab based on personality compatibility analysis.'

'Really? That's a bit sinister.'

Reims shrugged. 'A necessity of colony life. You spend that much time together, things will get ugly if you don't get along.'

'Does that work?'

'Most of the time. When it doesn't, there's ColPol.'

Connie glanced at the ColPol patch on Reims's therms. 'How's that working out for you?'

Reims sighed. 'If this works, I'm hoping Chief Smith will do the right thing.'

'And if he doesn't?' asked Connie.

'If he doesn't...' Reims frowned. Shit. She was going to have to make sure. 'I will make sure he does.'

Connie twisted around in her seat to face Reims properly. 'What do you mean?'

'I mean that I'll talk to Chief Smith and suggest that he does the right thing.'

'And he'll listen to you?'

'With a bit of encouragement.'

Reims checked the clock on the rover dashboard. 'She's been more than thirty minutes.' Thirty-one to be precise.

'I'm sure she's fine,' said Connie.

Reims checked the clock again. Thirty-two minutes. 'I'm going to make sure she's okay.'

Connie put a hand on Reims's arm. 'Give it a little more time.'

Reims took Connie's hand and lifted if off her arm. 'I'm going now. Come if you want.'

Connie looked Reims in the eye for a moment. 'Fine. Come on, let's go rescue your damsel in distress.'

Reims had to switch her cuff on to open the airlock. This had the side effect of announcing her presence on the colony network. It couldn't be helped.

The data centre was not a particularly big building. Miniaturisation had reduced the footprint of data storage significantly over the years. Reducing the size even more was the fact that all required cooling could be provided by the external heat sinks dumping heat into the cold martian atmosphere.

The main hall had several doors leading off it.

'Which one?' asked Connie.

'Not sure,' said Reims.

None of the doors were labelled except for 'EXIT' above the door they had come in.

Reims was about to pick one at random when she heard voices from behind the door on their left. She looked at

Connie and put her finger to her lips. Then she put her ear to the door. She recognised Josie's voice but she couldn't quite make out what she was saying.

'In here,' whispered Reims.

Reims readied her taser and nodded Connie towards the door handle.

Connie turned the handle and pushed the door open to reveal a large open plan office. Josie was standing near one of the desks in a heated discussion with a ColPol officer. She recognised him. Carver. What was he doing here?

Reims held her taser by her side and angled her body to keep the weapon out of sight. 'Hey, Carver.'

Carver looked up in surprise. 'Reims. Shit.'

The man was going for his taser. Well that answered one thing she had been wondering about. She was now wanted by ColPol after her little escapade in the agri-dome. Carver must be here to pick up Josie.

Reims raised and fired while Carver's taser was still clearing his holster. There was a buzz as the charge flowed down the wires, his muscles locked and he fell backwards over a desk, sending a monitor crashing to the floor.

'Holy shit,' said Josie.

'Have you done what you need to do?'

'Not quite. This guy interrupted me before I could finish.'

'Well hurry up.'

Carver was struggling to get to his feet. 'Reims, you bitch.'

Reims gave him another jolt then walked over and scooped Carver's taser off the floor. 'Thanks, my battery pack was getting low.'

Carver replied with an incoherent, pained gurgle.

Josie sat down at her desk and continued with the news feed setup, finishing by dramatically banging the enter key. 'There. Done. It will take a few seconds for the AI to insert it into a news item.'

'Time we were gone then.'

Reims pulled some tie-wraps from her pocket and secured Carver's hands behind his back. 'Sorry about this, Carver.'

'You won't get away with this,' said Carver. He seemed to have recovered the power of speech.

'Maybe. Maybe not. We'll see,' said Reims.

While they waited for the airlock to cycle, Josie was watching her cuff intently. 'There it is.' She turned the volume on her cuff up so the others could hear the AI newsreader's voice.

'—of a conspiracy at the highest levels of the colony council. The evidence has been made public and is available via a data-net link.'

'Oh boy,' said Josie.

'Now I need to make sure Smith does the right thing.' Reims activated her cuff and placed a call to chief Smith.

Smith's voice sounded annoyed. 'Reims. Where the hell have you been?'

'Upholding the law,' Reims said calmly.

'You're in serious trouble. You need to come back and turn yourself in.'

'I'm afraid that won't be possible. Have you seen the news feed, sir?'

'What the hell are you talking about?'

'You really should check it. I can wait.'

The call went quiet for a few moments. Reims waited impatiently. She knew that her cuff network log on was being traced and a response team would be on the way.

'Jesus Christ, Reims. What have you done?'

'I've made sure a law breaker will be brought to justice.'

'Webb? Are you crazy?'

'The truth is out now. There's no way this can be covered up.'

'We're going to have to bring him in.'

Reims could hear the dawning realisation in Smith's voice as he assimilated the implications of the very public exposure of the murders and cover-ups.

'I knew you would do the right thing.' She hadn't, but he didn't need to know that. 'Can I suggest Conway as the arresting officer?'

'Conway? Of course. That makes sense. What about you?'

'Consider this my resignation. Good bye, sir.'

'Resignation? What?' Smith sounded flustered.

Reims ended the call and switched off her cuff. 'That went better than expected.'

'That's it? We won?' asked Connie.

'As much as we can win,' said Reims.

'I don't think I'll be keeping my job at the data centre,' said Josie.

'And I've just retired from ColPol,' said Reims.

'I know a nice little hut you can move into,' said Connie. 'It has a great view of the lake.'

Josie's face lit up with excitement. 'A lake? Are you serious? What you waiting for? Let's go!'

CHAPTER 37

In the months since Connie, Reims and Josie had returned from their mission on Mars, the Box had been used to bring more people from Earth to the settlement on Kevs. It had not taken long for people to shorten the name 'Kev's world' to Kevs, and this had now become the official name for their new home. Kevin was glad, he had inwardly cringed every time anyone had used the name 'Kev's world'.

Although their farms could now produce enough food for everyone, they were still using the Box to fabricate electronics. Their own workshops were limited by a lack of raw materials. Some new arrivals had worked in the mining trade on Earth and were surveying for copper, silver, tin and other metals used in the manufacture of electronics. One site had been identified, and they were setting up operations there using equipment scavenged from Earth.

Kevin was here for a multimeter. He banged on the side of the Box in frustration. 'Let me in, dammit.'

Kevin had been trying for five minutes to get the circular 'door' to open in the side of the Box so he could fabricate the multimeter for Dimitri. He tried one more time. 'Box, open the door.'

Nothing. He gave the recalcitrant thing a good hard kick. Then hopped around on one foot swearing. He sat down, removed his boot and inspected his toes for damage.

'Morning, Kev. You got the multimeter?'

'No, I do not have the bloody multimeter.' Kevin jammed his foot back into his boot. 'Because this bloody box won't let me in.'

'Really? Let me try.'

Simone had instructed the Box to do what Dimitri said when she had reached the eighth month of her pregnancy. This had saved her having to hike out to the Box fetching supplies.

'Box, open the door,' said Dimitri confidently.

Nothing happened.

Dimitri tried again, shouting the instruction several times before giving up.

'I'm going to get Sim,' said Kevin.

As he approached Simone's hut, Kevin could hear the un-mistakable crying of a baby. He broke into a jog, quickly arriving at his destination.

He rapped his knuckles on the door. 'Sim?'

The door was opened by Diane, the settlement's midwife.

'Hello, Kevin.' She was smiling.

'Is she okay?' asked Kevin.

'Mother and baby are both fine,' said Diane.

The settlement huts all followed a similar design; a main living area and one or more connected bedrooms. Simone was in one of the single person dwellings.

Kevin knocked on the bedroom door. 'Sim?'

'Come in, Kev.'

Simone was sat up in her bed holding her baby. Kevin almost couldn't believe it. His sister was a mother. He was an uncle.

'Say hello to your nephew.'

'Shit. I mean, hello nephew.'

Simone held out the tiny baby. 'Come hold him.'

Kevin hesitantly took the baby into his arms and looked down at his wrinkled face. He jumped as the child's mouth opened and he started to cry loudly.

'You'd better have him back.' Kevin passed the precious charge back to his mother.

Simone comforted her son, gently cooing at him and rocking him until he settled down and was quiet.

'Have you chosen a name for him?' asked Kevin.

'Not yet. I wish he could meet his father,' said Simone.

Kevin didn't know what to say, so he said nothing.

Simone looked up at Kevin. 'I miss him Kev.'

Kevin sat on the edge of the bed and put an arm around her shoulders. 'I know, Sim.'

Simone looked down at her son and smiled. 'But this little guy. Oh, this little guy.'

Kevin couldn't help smiling along. 'He's a little miracle, Sim.'

'The second born Kevsian. Maybe he'll marry little Nadia when he grows up,' said Simone.

Nadia had been born a couple of months earlier, the child of one of the women rescued from Earth.

'We should have a big party, like we did for Nadia.'

'That's a great idea! Maybe we could start a new Kevsian tradition.'

'I'll get started now.' Kevin stood up. 'Oh. I almost forgot. We're having trouble getting into the Box. I was going to ask you to come and try, but it can wait.'

'Trouble?'

'It's not opening for me or Dimitri.'

'That's worrying. Give me half an hour and I'll be with you.'

'Should you be moving around?' asked Kevin.

'Kevin. Let me be the judge of if or if not I can do anything.'

'Sorry, Sim. I'll get back and let Dimitri know.'

Kevin was relieved when Simone showed up at the Box forty minutes later. Dimitri had started swearing and throwing rocks at the Box. So far it hadn't retaliated.

'Bastard.' Dimitri bounced another rock off the side without making a mark.

'That's not going to help,' said Simone.

Dimitri stepped to one side with an exaggerated bow. 'Please. Get the damn thing to open.'

Simone ignored him. 'Box, open the door.'

Nothing happened.

Simone tried again. 'Box, open the door.'

Nothing happened again.

'Oh shit,' said Kevin.

'I agree,' said Simone.

'I suppose we should get the alien-tech team to take a look,' said Kevin.

'That bunch of idiots?' asked Dimitri. 'They've been messing around at the alien facility for months and got nowhere.'

'They may have some insight,' said Simone. 'I'll talk to Philip.'

* * *

Philip Hargreaves had moved most of the research camp from outside the alien facility to outside the Box. That had been a week ago.

Simone and Kevin were sitting on the grass while they watched Philip and another man taking pictures of the Box with thermal imaging cameras. Kevin wondered what they expected to see that they hadn't seen already.

'Well, I guess that's it then,' said Simone.

'What's what?' asked Kevin.

'We're stranded here. No more trips to Earth or Mars.'

'Oh. Yes.'

He'd come to that conclusion himself after Philip and his team had replicated their success with the alien facility by making zero progress with getting back into the Box. To all intents and purposes it was now a giant, inert grey cube.

'We'll have to tell the others,' said Simone.

'I think they already know,' said Kevin.

'You're probably right.' Simone stood up and brushed grass from the seat of her trousers. 'Dimitri is holding a soy-burger barbecue to celebrate the naming of the settlement. You coming?'

'Is Connie going?' asked Kevin.

'I think so. After all, the name was her idea.' Simone smiled.

'Good. Let's go eat,' said Kevin.

Epilogue

Raphael left Nadia behind as he sprinted through the winding streets of New Akpoort.

He streaked past his aunt and uncle's house, hurdling the plastic bins at the end of a gravel path that led to the porch.

He heard his aunt Connie call after him. 'Hello, Raphael!'

He waved an arm above his head in acknowledgement and continued his run towards the centre of the town. He slowed as he reached the large grey cube that dominated the central square. He wasn't even breathing heavily after the run from the lakeside. Physical activity came very easily to him; his mother told him it was his special heritage.

He tried to decide where he should stand for maximum nonchalance while he waited for Nadia to catch up with him. He walked over to the monument and put his hand on the smooth grey surface, intending to adopt a cool looking pose like one of the actors in the movies he watched with his grandfather.

Raphael snatched his hand back in shock as a circular

opening flicked into existence with a high pitched 'ting'. The interior was brightly lit, and he could see a table, chairs, a sofa and even the shiny black surface of a wall screen. This was beyond weird.

'Raph, what are you doing?' Nadia had arrived.

'It just opened. Come on, let's go inside.'

'Are you sure it's safe?' asked Nadia.

'No. But how dangerous can it be? It's got a comfy sofa.'

'Shouldn't we go and tell our parents?'

'Maybe you're right. It opened quickly. I suppose it could close as fast.' As soon as he thought about the hole closing, the opening swiftly shrank until it disappeared, leaving the featureless surface as it was before.

'Oh!' exclaimed Nadia.

'That was weird,' said Raphael.

He wished it had stayed open so he could take a look inside.

The 'ting' sounded again, and the hole was back.

Smiling, Raphael held his hand out to Nadia. 'You coming to explore?'

ABOUT THE AUTHOR

Before realising he'd rather write books instead of code, Richard spent twenty years working as a software engineer. During this time Richard also indulged in socialising through tabletop roleplaying; often as the Gamesmaster and often with a pint of ale! From this was born his passion for, and enjoyment of, storytelling. Richard now spends his days writing and visiting various locations during this pursuit. Officially the local library and, unofficially, the local pub.

Printed in Great Britain
by Amazon

32999173R00153